# SECRETS AND SHADOWS

BEAUTIFUL BEASTS ACADEMY

KIM FAULKS

MILA YOUNG

*Mila and I would love to dedicate this to the readers. For those who stuck with us, and who fell in love with two quirky characters. Thank you from the bottom of our heart.*

*Mila and Kim, a.k.a Kila Foung*

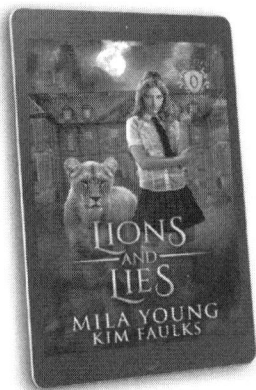

Grab your FREE book and start the Beautiful Beasts Academy Series today!

*There's nothing like a witch storm to unearth a century of dark secrets…and there's nothing like a best friend with a flaming sword at your back to end them once and for all…*

The curse which infected those I love is over…and the woman in black is now gone.
But Bastias Academy has changed since the Witch storm.
Secrets have resurfaced and shadows consume the dorms.
An old Principal haunts the hallways, leaving grave dirt in her wake.
But that's not all that's surfaced.
The fish in the pond are savaged and eaten….
And one is mysteriously gone.
A monsterous golden fish with bright yellow eyes, leaving behind human shaped footprints in its wakc.
Ava takes refuge with Chuck, leaving me to huddle with the Wolves.
And as love and lust lunger on Judas' lips I find myself drawn into a battle like nothing before.
Lions will come.
Lies will be exposed.
But will love conquer all?
I guess I'm about to find out.

# CHAPTER ONE

## WHO YOU GONNA CALL?

The squeal of bedsprings howled through my room, tearing me from the dream. But Judas' arms still waited for me, and his lips whispered of things he wanted to do to my body. I groaned and rolled over, tugging the blankets higher. "Too early, Ava. Go back to your own room."

Still, she never answered...

*Creeeeaaakkkk. Creak...creeeaaakkk...*

"Ava, I swear to Lucifer, I'm gonna hurt you," I mumbled.

"Don't mind me, honey," an unfamiliar voice filled the room. "It's gonna take me a good hour to get my hair just right."

Someone's feet landed on the floor with a *thump*. I cracked open my eyes to see a grimy, moth-eaten, hot pink skirt over black tights. I opened my eyes wider as she strode past my bed and made for the bathroom. Well, I thought it was a *her*. I wasn't really sure. I couldn't see anything but a rat's nest head of hair that stank like a gallon of hairspray billowing out behind her.

I shoved up from the bed and shook my head as the off-tune sound of Cyndi Lauper belted out about how Girls just Wanna have Fun, and then the singing suddenly stopped.

"You know, I was like totally having the strangest dream," the stranger called out from my bathroom before she stepped into the doorway. She was pale...like ghostly pale with dark sunken eyes that seemed to pierce mine. "I saw your friend totally wiggin' out while you and her were carrying a dead body down the stairs to hide it not far from where I was chained."

*"Ahhh..."* I scrambled from the bed and stared at this stranger. "W-who the Hell are you?"

Thick metal shackles hung from her wrists, the links severed in two.

"Don't you know, honey?" Pale lips stretched into a wide smile until they split. "I'm Cassidy, and this here's my room."

I shoved backwards and then turned at the last minute, lunging for my door as a scream cut through the air. I whipped my gaze toward the sound as Ava screeched, *"Get out! Get all the way fucking OUT!"*

The hallway darkened as I stepped into it, shadows reaching wide, closing in like a fist around me. I grabbed Ava's door handle and pushed, slipping inside.

A hairbrush sailed past me, narrowly missing me by an inch before it smashed into the wall. Something *oozed*...and laughter floated from the doorway. It wasn't human or immortal for that matter.

It wasn't even matter...just a *glob* with beady black eyes and a wicked sneer.

"Ava?"

*"That thing saw my bits!"* she howled over the hiss of the shower. *"It leered at me!"*

Anger lashed inside me at the injustice. "Why, you little..."

"Little?" The *thing* jeered and grabbed its chest, jiggling things that looked like boobs. "*Thank you.* But I'll show you mine, if you show me yours?"

I gagged at the sight and swallowed my revulsion before cocking my fist. "Get the Hell out!"

"Oh." The thing pouted...*it actually pouted,* and then jumped up with a grin, and blew the biggest raspberry in my face before it called over its shoulder. "I've seen bigger pimples on my butt than those titties!"

"Arrrggghhhh!" Ava tore from the bathroom, clutching a towel to her soapy body, her hair tucked up under a plastic shower cap. "I will take you to the deepest *Goddamn depths and leave you there!*"

But the thing was gone, slipping *through* the damn wall. Like it'd never been there at all.

"Mor," whimpered Ava as she dripped on the carpet. "What the fuck was that thing?"

"Looked like a poltergeist to me," came an unwelcome voice behind me.

I jumped and spun as the ghost girl, Cassidy, waltzed into Ava's room and looked my best friend up and down. "Yup, that's you...the girl who wigged out."

Faint screams came from somewhere outside as I turned to Ava. "I think something is really...really wrong here."

"Ah, no shit Sherlock." Ava just spun and strode to the bathroom, giving me full view of her ass. "I'm going to finish my damn shower."

I stared after her as the shower door opened and closed once more, and then turned to the ghost girl. Only when I looked, she didn't exactly look like a ghost. "I, ah, think we got off on the wrong foot there."

"If memory serves me right, it was a hand," she answered, and then cocked her head when I said nothing. "You know." She lifted a hand, smacked her boob and then waved her hands in the air. *"Ahhh,* it touched my boob!"

I swallowed hard as the room spun.

"How's that?" She smiled as I just turned and yanked open Ava's door.

"I thought it was pretty accurate," she rambled on, following me as I strode back along the darkened hallway and into my room.

"Hey!" Came a howl from Nesrin's room, followed by a savage snarl. "Get out of my damn toilet!"

The plasma looking blob flew through the wall of Nesrin's room and into the hallway, dripping with what could only be toilet water.

"That's gross," I snarled and strode into my room.

Cassidy was hot on my tail, slamming the door into the glob-thing's face as it came for us.

"Look." I spun and met her head on. "I don't know you. I'm sure there's some serious misunderstanding."

She just lifted her hand and tugged at the once white lace of her fingerless gloves. "No misunderstanding."

I was getting nowhere with her. "Just stay away from me." Then I turned and yanked open my cupboard door and grabbed a clean uniform.

I thought the terror was over...thought that the Witch storm last night had ended everything, including the curse that plagued those I loved. But this place was going to Hell in a handbasket, a poltergeist riddled, 80's ridden Hell.

I marched into the bathroom and closed the door as my roommate lifted her hand and took a step toward me. "Hey, I need my hairsp—"

The bathroom door closed with a *bang.* I flipped the

lock and just stood there for a second, wondering what in the world had happened. Girls with shackles for bracelets, and ghoulish looking blobs that liked to spy on girls in the shower.

A maniacal laugh floated faintly through the walls. I just stepped away and hurried to the shower, hitting the taps. "I'll wash in my damn underwear. Yes, Sir."

I placed my uniform on the cabinet and then watched the walls as I yanked my nightie over my head and hugged my body, covering my breasts with my hands.

The idea worked, until I realized I needed my hands to wash. *"Ugh!"*

I kept one eye on the wall and the other on what I was doing as I washed and scrubbed and then hit the taps once more, cutting off the stream. Squeals and screams still drifted in from somewhere outside as I dried myself and yanked on clean clothes.

"I just want to make sure we're on the same page here." Cassidy lifted a finger as I pushed past her on my way out of the bathroom. "I'm not a snitch. I don't plan on telling anyone you killed that poor human and hid his body in the basement."

I spun and glared at her. "I didn't kill him...I didn't kill anyone. I was set up, *okay?* By another Vampire wanting to get rid of my family. So yeah, I hid the body until I could figure out who set me up."

"Oh, okay, *dramatic much?*" She rose a brow.

I just stilled, closed my eyes and inhaled hard while I counted to five, and then turned and sat on the end of my bed while I yanked my socks and shoes on.

"Man, the dress code here has gotten super *ugly.*"

*Gotten super ugly?* I just couldn't win. I grabbed my bag and my brush and yanked open the door, stepping out into the hallway at the same time as Ava. She whipped a thunderous gaze toward me and then turned her gaze to the glass doors of the foyer below as a girl ran past the front of our dorm screaming at the top of her lungs.

"What the fuck, Mor?" my best friend whispered.

I took a step at the same time as she did, edging to the top of the stairs and then slowly descended to the foyer.

"Hey, wait for me," Nesrin called from above and hurried down the stairs after us. "No way in Hell are you leaving me alone. This is some freaky goddamn shit, Livingstone."

I nodded and edged toward the dorm door. If I thought the curse and the Witch storm was bad, this was another level of crazy.

Ava opened the door, waiting a second before taking a tentative step outside. The dark, broody sky seemed to bluster above us.

Nesrin ducked and ran, sprinting with long strides toward the main building. Ava looked at me, gave a shrug and then followed, bounding for the main doors. There was no way in Hell I was being left behind.

I took off after her, catching up and then overtaking her about halfway. Suddenly something came from the sky, tearing past, screaming like a damn banshee. I cowered, throwing one hand over my head and yanked open the door with the other.

Ava rushed past me and stumbled inside, sweeping her hair into some semblance of normalcy and stomping her feet. "Ugh, what in the world was that?"

"That," Nesrin growled and stared down the corridor. "Is what happens when a Hellhound's in damn charge."

She strode forward as the fluorescent lights dimmed and flickered overhead.

"A dead body. Power-riddled diamonds, and a damn curse. What the Hell is next?" Ava growled and strode after her.

And as she left me behind, I had a horrible feeling...we were about to find out.

# CHAPTER TWO

### AN UNLIKELY ALLY

"Hurry, hurry, take your seats," Ms. Truro said, waving us into her classroom.

Ava and I slid into two available seats in the middle of the room, plonking our oversized textbooks on the tables. Ava shuffled closer to me and leaned over.

"I feel like we've just stepped into Ghostbusters this morning," she whispered. "Maybe we need proton packs to get rid of the invaders." She sniggered to herself, seeming to enjoy all the ghostly activity, which was the opposite of her reaction this morning with the peeping Tom ghost in her bathroom.

"You actually liked that movie?" I asked.

Ava's mouth dropped open. "You didn't just say that? If you haven't watched that movie, then you're dead to me. It's only *the* best ghost movie out there. It has everything, from a Keymaster, spirits taking over the city, and a fridge demon."

"Fridge demon, really? So he ate all the cheese and that makes him scary?" I giggled to myself as Ava glared my way.

"We're watching that movie tonight," she threatened.

"Plus, technically it's not a fridge demon, but more of a portal into Hell."

"Pretty sure I can see my fair share of ghosts around campus."

"Are you two quite finished," Ms. Truro snapped.

We glanced up to find our teacher in front of the class, tapping her toe, and everyone else looking our way too.

Judas, Nero and Bond were sitting across the room and I smiled their way, adoring the way they looked at me. But if they were near us, I was certain they'd agree with me on Ghostbusters.

A guy's hand shot up from the front of the class and even before the teacher looked at him, he started talking. "Why are there ghosts at the Academy? A girl in an ancient ballgown was sleeping in bed with me this morning and scared me half to death."

Everyone's hand jutted up, all of them asking similar questions, the chatter deafening. Ava cut me a look as she mouthed the word, *Ghostbusters*.

A sudden explosion of wind rushed into the room out of nowhere, tearing at our hair, clothes, and books. I scrambled for my textbook as it slid off the table and drew it to my chest, holding it tight against the hurricane as my hair flew in every direction. Books and papers were tossed about the room, an empty chair skidded across the floor.

A prickling sensation of magic danced on my skin.

"What the hell's happening?" Ava was already hunched under her table.

"Enough!" Ms. Truro lowered her raised hands and the wind died. We didn't have many witches at school, but the several we did, including this teacher, were not to be messed with.

No one said a word and only the shuffling of paper and scraping of chairs sounded as everyone settled back down.

"Until Principal Balefire advises us on the situation, classes go on as normal, and I don't teach about spirits and ghouls. Open your book to chapter seven. Rare breeds is the topic for today."

Half the class groaned, and like the rest of them, I longed to know what was going on. Then again, not much seemed to surprise me when it came to Bestias Academy.

The next hour dragged until I spotted movement in the window and glance over to see the spirit from my room peering into the class, only her eyes and spiked hair sticking above the window frame. Geez, she wasn't subtle at all. And how much spray did she use to keep so much hair upright like that?

Her gaze met mine and she gave me a small wave. Instinctively, I waved back but dropped my hand just as fast. *What am I doing?*

Ava was studying me, her brows pulled together with confusion. She looked at the window, the ghost girl now gone, and back to me. "You okay?"

I nodded. "Dandy."

While Ms. Truro read out a passage from the book about how most shifters could successfully mate with others, the door to the room swung open with a loud thud.

I jumped in my seat, as did Ava and most of the students.

The teacher stuck her hand out, a spark of electricity shooting out from her fingers and colliding into the young student who'd burst into the room. He froze mid step, and now stood in front of the entire class with his eyes and mouth gaping open, his arms frozen in a swinging motion by his sides, and balancing on one foot. He reminded me of a flamingo.

"What is the meaning of this?" the teacher approached him and with the snap of her fingers, he collapsed out of the freeze, gasping for breath, and fell to his knees.

He mumbled something between his wheezing breath.

"Speak up, boy."

"The fish...the fish at the back pond, they're all dead," he finally blurted.

*What was he talking about?*

"Mr. Jacobson, if this is a prank..." She gripped her hips.

"No." He cleared his throat and shook his head. "No prank Miss...they're all dead outside the water."

Ava flinched, and then jerked her gaze toward Salome. I followed the movement, the nagging feeling of a dream blooming. Something passed between them, a *knowing* I wasn't part of.

Salome was pale, hands clenched around the edges of her desk as she shook her head and whispered. "No." She turned her head, meeting Ava's gaze.

And in a second Ava shoved her chair backwards and rose to stand.

"Sit down, Ms. Blaine," the teacher snapped.

But there was no stopping Ava as she knocked into the desk and stumbled toward the doorway.

Salome was on her heels.

"What's going on?" Judas muttered from across the room.

I could only shake my head. "I have no idea."

There had been fear in Ava's eyes. She was hiding something from me and this wasn't the first time I'd had this feeling. I gripped my desk, rising to stand.

"Ms Livingstone. Back to your seat this *instant!*" Ms. Truro barked.

"Ava!" I jerked my gaze toward the open door. But she was gone, tearing through the door, Salome after her, leaving the thud of footsteps behind.

"Well, someone seems to care more about the fish in the pond then they do for their assignment. Leave, Mr. Jacobson, before I have you hanging from the rafters."

The poor boy hurried from the room, stammering and shaking, but I couldn't tear my gaze from the door. Where did Ava go so quickly, and why did Salome go after her?

I shot my hand up. "Miss, maybe we should all go and investigate the pond?"

Her eyes narrowed at me and with a flick of her hand, the door to the room shut with a bang. "No one is going to the pond during *my* class."

I cursed under my breath, flinching as a shattering scream came from outside. All heads turned toward the sound, some of the students shot from their chairs and stumbled to the far wall of the classroom.

"What in the name of his dark lord is it now?" the teacher snapped.

Heavy footsteps echoed, two...three...four different sounds blended into one thunderous sound. There was a roar, and then a *thud* against the wall from outside. A picture of an Ancient bounced and then fell with a *crash* against the floor.

I lunged from my seat at the same time as Judas.

*"Wait!"* Ms. Truro yelled.

But we were already running. Judas slowed for a second, letting me through the door first, and then followed close behind. I didn't need to look over my shoulder to know Bond and Nero were there.

There was a roar as I stepped through the doorway. A blur of white behind a wall of Hellhounds, and for a second. I didn't understand what I was seeing as one of the guards' feet left the floor before he was pitched backwards through the air.

He hit the wall with a *crack,* and fell to the floor.

Laughter cut through the air, chilling, glee-filled laughter that made the hairs on my arms stand on end.

Between the thick trunks of Hellhounds came a small girl, dressed in a filthy white pinafore with a frilly pale blue shirt underneath. She ducked, slipped through one of the guard's legs and popped out behind them.

*"Tada!"* She spread her arms wide and then turned to smile at me.

Her face was pale...nails blackened and broken, like she'd been clawing at something...clawing and clawing...

"I'm free now!" She danced and spun, before melting into nothing. "I'm freeee...."

"Hells bells," Judas whispered.

I glanced at him, and then looked to the burly guard who slowly picked himself up off the floor.

"Did you see the way she..." The Alpha stepped closer.

"I saw." I kept on moving, keeping my back to the wall as I skirted the Hellhound. "I saw only too well."

I hurried past the lockers and the cafeteria to the doors that led to the back of the main building. There were students already cramming the doorway, gagging and crying, staring out with hands over their mouths.

"Let me through." I tried to slip between them, twisting my body to scrape my spine against the doorway.

"Come on," Judas snarled. "Let us through."

"Salome?" Nesrin called from just in front of me. She

shoved a hand between the bodies and shoved them aside. *"Salome!"*

The foul stench of rotting fish made me retch. I slapped my hand to cover my nose and pushed just like Nesrin. "Sorry...*please, so sorry."*

And inch by inch I came closer. Dried scales glinted between the legs of a girl. I reached out, grasping her shoulder and pushed her aside. Ava stood on the other side of the pond next to Salome, both stared at the mangled fish carcases. Fins flayed open, tails still. Bite marks in their flesh, some with gaping wounds.

"The cat shifters have done this!" someone cried out.

I caught the flinch from Ava as Salome lifted her gaze to mine.

"They did this! They need to be chained up!" another followed.

And the cries for retribution echoed through the crowd.

"She did it!" A ghoul lifter a hand and pointed at Nesrin.

Nesrin's dark eyes flashed with anger. I wouldn't put it past the Panther, and no one knew her as well as me. I'd seen her anger, felt her rage, but I'd also seen her sincerity, and as much as I hated to admit it, she'd changed.

"I did not do this!" Nesrin stabbed a finger at the ground where the dead fish lay. "Stop staring at me. *I didn't do this."*

*"Ennnouugghh!"* The savage growl boomed through the air, making everyone flinch.

As Balefire strode through the doorway, the sea of students parted like he was a God. He never once looked at them, never once lifted his gaze until he neared. Orange flames danced in his eyes as they met mine.

His lips curled, baring a hint of white teeth before he

cast that hatred toward the mass of fish carcasses on the ground. "No one is pointing *any* fingers," he snapped.

Some of the students slowly drifted away, not wanting to be in his firing line. But it seemed that no matter what I did I was the bullseye.

Ava pushed through those who remained, and Salome followed. Nesrin watched them, staring at the Lion-shifter. But both her and my best friend stared at the ground, looking for...*something*.

When I finally reached them, I stepped with them, searching the ground before Salome lifted a hand and motioned to a mark on the ground. Balefire knelt near the pond and skimmed his fingers through the water. I watched him from the corner of my eye, just as he watched us.

"What is it?" I hissed as Salome knelt and pressed her finger to a mark on the ground.

Nesrin came closer, and then the Wolves, until we had a wall of protection.

"Fin marks," Salome muttered. "Here...and then here."

I followed the lines in the dirt until they suddenly changed.

"That's no fin mark," Judas growled.

"No, it isn't." I lifted my gaze as Salome rose from the ground.

She glanced at Ava, and then with a sigh gave a nod.

"We have something to tell you." My best friend met my gaze. "Something that happened before you came to Bestias Academy, and you're not going to like it."

# CHAPTER THREE

### BLIND MAN ON A GALLOPING HORSE

THE LODGE WAS THE ONLY HALF-WAY SANE PART OF the Academy with dark corners and a crackling fire, but the students seemed to be avoiding the place. Maybe they were too busy running and screaming, being chased by who knew what.

I glanced at the empty sofas and tables and then turned down the hallway to the sitting room. Shadows moved against the glowing fireplace. I felt the first faint flickers of warmth as I stepped through.

Ava lifted her head to look at me, Salome stood next to her, taking comfort. The sight so alien, like I'd somehow stepped into an alternate reality.

Judas and the Wolves stood next to the fireplace. Nesrin sat on a sofa at the edge of the amber glow watching everyone with guarded eyes. "Well? You brought us here, what's so damn important?"

Ava glanced at Salome and gave her a nod. "This is your story."

Yellow eyes flickered and danced with the glow of the fire as Salome took a deep breath. "I was never meant to start this Academy. I was never meant to know you, or anything here. I'm not who you think I am. I'm a thief...I'm a rogue. I stole something that belonged to my father before my Uncle had him killed. Ava...Ava found me just outside of this building, bleeding and hurt. She helped me, saved me. Those fin marks outside the pond...well, they're not from any fish. They're from one of my Uncle's pack, sent to take back this...and kill me."

She lifted her hand and nestled between her fingers was the biggest yellow stone I'd ever seen. Everyone stared, including Nesrin.

"Wait," the Panther muttered and shoved to stand. "You're telling me your name's not Salome?"

She heaved a long exhale, her shoulders curving forward, her expression filled with sadness. "Yes, that part's real, everything else you know about me is a lie," Salome answered, her voice soft like admitting the truth hurt.

Nesrin stared at her for a long time and I could see the flash of betrayal, even felt it a little before she spoke. "And what, you thought you couldn't come to me with this? That I'd, what...tell everyone?"

"At first, yeah, I thought you might."

I winced at the sting of truth.

"And then I got to know you. And Brylee too, and I saw she was using you, hurting you, and through you, others." Salome glanced my way then back to Nesrin. "That wasn't you, I know that. But I had to keep quiet, I hope you understand?"

Somehow, I felt like she was talking to me too.

"But now he's out there." Salome looked to the hallway. "And it's only a matter of time before my Uncle comes for me."

"Then let him come," Nesrin snarled, white teeth

flashed with the curl of her lips. "You think I'm going to stand by and let someone hurt you?"

She glanced my way, as though she was waiting for something. Was this a peace offering?

"Me too." I took a step forward and relief swept across Ava's face. Her lips curved into a smile.

"And us." Judas lifted his gaze from the fireplace.

"And it looks like me as well," a deep baritone growled behind us.

I jumped at the sound and spun. Chuck was there with arms crossed, leaning against the wall. He glanced at Ava. I knew the real reason why he was weighing in on this fight and it had nothing to do with golden stones and murderous Uncles.

"Then it's decided." Nesrin glanced around the room. "Salome, you're bunking with me."

"In your room you mean?" The Lioness jerked her gaze toward the Alpha female.

"You have any other suggestions? Unless you want to share a room with Ava and her pervy Poltergeist or Mor and her weird new roomie with the strange look and shackles around her wrist."

"I'm good," Salome answered in a rush.

"Good." Nesrin nodded and then folded her arms. "Now, seeing as though we have everything out in the open now, we should be heading back to class. Unless you have more nasty secrets you want to tell us."

The Panther looked at me when she said it. And here I was thinking she'd finally turned a new leaf. Maybe she had. Maybe the golden yellow leaf was nice on one side, but underneath it was shit brown. "You know, I was actually starting to like you," I snarled and took the first step.

"Can't have that happening, can we?" There was a

spark of something akin to satisfaction in her eyes as I shook my head and kept on walking. Ava hurried after me, winding her arm through mine before we hit the entrance to the library.

"You know," she leaned close to murmur. "I think I love you more and more every damn day."

I smiled at her, and clasped my hand over hers. We might've started off as friends, but we were closer than that now. We were family.

We walked into class like that, her arm wound through mine. The other students were still talking about the dead fish and who'd killed them, but now I knew the truth, I knew it was a cat shifter who'd killed them—just one in particular.

"Okay, quiet down," Mr. Bloise muttered and flinched as something hit the glass window from outside.

We were all jumpy, and had good reason to be. Still we tried to concentrate, flinching with every *thump* from outside, until finally the bell rang.

Class after class was the same, until finally we shoved up from our desks at the last bell.

"I feel exhausted," I muttered and heaved my pack over my shoulder.

"Me too. Meet you in the dorm?"

Ava glanced my way, waiting for a second until I nodded.

"Sure."

Then she was gone, slipping between the crowd as they shoved through the doorway to get out of here. I could never understand that herd mentality, it wasn't like they were going far.

"Here." Bond grasped my pack. "Let me carry that for you."

I smiled at him, meeting the warmth in his eyes before turning to Nero and then Judas. "Thank you. You're so good to me."

And that sexy dream from this morning drifted to the surface.

"You okay?" Nero murmured, his brow furrowed, blue eyes blazing.

*Hell, he was gorgeous.*

There was a twitch of his lips, before they curled into a smile, and I was seized by that sexy tug of his mouth.

Judas just chuckled and shook his head before he started for the door. "One day, Livingstone. One day you're gonna drop those walls."

I followed him out, as Bond and Nero laughed and jostled behind me until we reached my dorm.

"See you soon?" Judas leaned close.

I felt myself gravitate to him, that dead *thing* inside my chest shuddering with life. "Yeakay. I mean, yes."

"And okay." He tried to fight the smirk and lost.

*Yeakay? What an idiot.*

"You know what I meant." I shook my head and play-fully gave him a punch to the shoulder.

He played the part, stumbling and grasping his arm. *"Ouch, that hurt."*

I could only laugh and watch them stride away, acting like goofs.

Loveable goofs...

*Crap, did I just think that?*

I turned, pushed through the dorm door and listened for anything unusual. But it was unusually quiet, so I walked up the stairs, my mind on the Wolves and their playful banter, until movement at the end of the hall stilled me at the top of the landing.

All I saw was Chuck, his arm up, braced against the wall, leaning into shadows. His white dress shirt was pulled taught around thick muscles, corded tight with the strain.

I took a step. "Chuck...you okay?"

He pulled back slowly, and then turned with the strangest look on his face. "I'm fine, sorry...I lost track of time."

And out of the shadows came Ava, cheeks flushed, lips just as red. I swallowed hard, glancing from her, to my bodyguard. He ran a hand through his hair, avoiding my gaze, and took a step away from her. "I'd better let you two get ready for dinner then."

And with a nod of his head he glanced at Ava once more, before slinking toward the stairs with his gaze to the ground.

"Okkkayyyy." Ava looked anywhere else but at me. "I'm just going to—"

"Stop right there," I demanded.

She froze as the heavy thud of Chuck's footsteps faded.

Her cheeks reddened, chest rose in shuddered breaths as the foyer door opened and then swung shut.

"So, this is...serious?" I started.

"I wasn't planning on you finding out like this," she started. "I wasn't hiding, but it just happened."

"And you think, what? That I was going to be pissed?"

"Upset, yeah, a little."

"Why?" I took a step closer. "You two are meant to be, even a blind man on a galloping horse could see that."

Surprise filled her eyes, and then she smiled...*no*, she *beamed*. "You really think so?"

"I know so." I stepped toward her and held out my arms. "And I couldn't be happier."

She exhaled hard, blowing my hair. "Hell, I was so

worried you were going to be upset. I'd never want to hurt you, you know that, right?"

I hugged her tight. "I know."

"Then dump your bag in your room and let's go eat, cause I'm starving," she murmured in my ear as a *thud* came from behind the door to the basement.

I watched the damn basement door and walked to my door. Screaming ghosts and damn banshees, I wanted out of here before something worse came through that door.

The scrape of nails on wood made me flinch. I shoved open my door, threw my bag toward the bed.

*"Oh, hey!"* My roommate looked up from reading a book on her bare mattress.

But I was out of there before I could answer, yanking the door closed and grabbing Ava's hand as we squealed like damn school girls and ran for our lives.

"Ain't no way," Ava huffed as we punched through the foyer door and stumbled outside. "I'm sleeping in that place. Look, I love you and everything, but the moaning and the screaming I can get at Chuck's." She stiffened, and then grinned.

"Get out." I shoved her and shook my head. "I'm trying to get the image of that out of my head."

She just laughed, tormenting me with kissy noises as we headed to the cafeteria.

"You really going to stay there, huh?"

"You okay with that?" She glanced my way.

"Yeah, of course. Just don't do anything I wouldn't do." The joke was lame.

"But you don't do anything, so where's the fun in that?" She laughed.

I smiled and nodded as we strode into the dining hall

and grabbed our food, me a blood shake and her...fish...*again*.

But her words stayed with me, even after we'd scraped our plates and headed back to the dorm.

"You going to get your things?" I motioned toward the doorway.

"I, ah, already have them at Chuck's."

She looked sheepish when I glanced her way, so I didn't push the point. She turned and gave me a quick hug. "Goodnight. Be careful, okay? If you need me...*us,* just call."

Then she was gone...and I swore I saw her skip.

I shoved through the dorm's front door. My boots were heavier than I remembered as I trudged up the stairs. A scrape came from the other side of the basement door once more. I stilled with the key in the lock of my room and waited.

*"You...come closer...."* came a voice on the other side of the basement door.

"Oh, *Hell no,"* I muttered, shoved my door wide and rushed inside. "Can't stay," I gushed as my new roommate swung her legs over the side of the mattress. "I got a...*thing.*"

I grabbed my bag of toiletries, pajamas and my pillow and raced for the door.

*But you don't do anything, so where's the fun in that?*

Ava's words haunted me as I hurried from my dorm to another. I pushed through their door and gripped my pillow, racing across the foyer to the sounds of male laughter. And with my heart crawling into my throat...I raised my knuckles to the door...*and knocked.*

# CHAPTER FOUR

## A GREAT BIG PUPPY PILE

The door to Judas' room was yanked open, but the Alpha was still busy laughing and talking to others. Finally, he muttered. "Yeah?" And swung his gaze to me. Confusion crowded in, carving a line between his brown as he looked at me, and then the pillow in my grasp. "Mor? What's wrong. You okay?"

"I can't stay there." *Please...please don't make this weird.* "There's something scratching the inside of the basement door and I... I have a weird new roommate that sings Aha and thinks this is still the eighties." He flinched, but I wasn't sure which part disturbed him the most. "Is it okay if I..."

I glanced at Nero as he shoved from Judas' bed, Bond followed, crowding the Alpha's back.

Hope flared in their gaze, and it was echoed in their Alpha as Judas stepped to the side and reached for my pillow. "Yeah of course...nurries...*I mean no worries.*"

"Nurries?" I smiled as he tripped over his own words.

And for once a blush crept through his cheeks. "Yeah, you know what I meant."

Bond grabbed my bag, as Nero closed the door to his

bedroom and then turned. They just stood there, staring at me...in their room, like I was a complete stranger.

"What?" I lifted my hand and touched my temple. "Have I grown a second head?"

"W-what?" Judas stammered. "No."

"No," Nero echoed.

"Nope, all good," Bond murmured, glancing at me from the corner of his eye.

No, this wasn't awkward at all.

"You guys are being weird. I'm getting some chocolate bars." I dropped my toiletry bag on the end of his bed and yanked open the door once more.

"Wait, not too many," Judas was hot on my heels. "Let me get it."

Nero came from out of nowhere, shoving Judas aside. "It's all good. I got this."

Coins clattered in their hands as they rushed toward the vending machine. Bond shoulder barged Nero, sending the other Beta Wolf flying.

"Nero!" I lunged for him, but the Wolf caught the stumble in an instant and was lunging toward Bond.

Nero tackled him, driving Bond to the ground with a grunt. Arms and legs went flying. Savage snarls turned into laughter as they rolled and wrestled along the entire foyer floor.

Bond shot up, lunging, before Nero caught his foot and dragged him back down to crash with a *thud*.

"Are they always like this?" I glanced to Judas who just watched them with a look of pride.

"Pretty much, yeah," he chuckled.

They seemed to have lost sight of the real reason we were out here in the first place. But I hadn't. I needed chocolate like I needed blood in this moment. So I stepped over the two tussling Wolves and swiped my card.

Nero slid his head out from underneath Bond's arm to watch me as I punched the buttons and the dark chocolate bar dropped to the bottom of the machine.

"I wanted to get that for you," he muttered and pushed against Bond's ribs.

*"Ooff,"* the blond Beta grunted.

"Well, you're too busy getting cosy with Bond, weren't you?" I yanked the bar free and tore the top of the wrapping with the point of my fangs.

They all watched me like they'd never seen a Vampire eat before.

"I'd like to see more of those fangs," Judas murmured, staring as I chomped down on the end of the chocolate.

"A few more of these and you just might." I waved the chocolate in his face.

Then there was a flurry of movement as all three Wolves scurried to swipe their cards and shove coins into the machine, stabbing buttons like their lives depended on it.

The poor machine whirled and the arms buzzed across the shelves like terminator had come to life with a bad case of PMS.

I just giggled, shook my head and made for the room. There was a *thud,* followed by a steady stream of cursing. The vending machine was rocked and cries of, "Did you get it? Reach *further. Put your whole damn arm in…"*

My belly jumped and twitched with laughter as I closed the door and made for the bed. It smelled like them, deep and musky, like a hunter…like a Wolf.

Judas opened the door and they all tumbled inside,

watching me as I crossed my ankles and finished the rest of my bar.

Ten more chocolate bars dropped from their hands and onto the bed.

There was an exhausted gasp of breath before Judas motioned to the array of goodies. "Take your pick."

I realized I hadn't once thought about the ghosts, or the new roommate, or even the curse. I was happy, *really happy*. It felt so...free.

Nero closed the bedroom door and Bond stepped forward, taking the empty wrapping from my fingers as Judas slowly reached over and grasped my hand, lifting chocolate covered fingers to his mouth.

"You can sleep here for as long as you want." He opened his mouth and slid my finger inside.

My body clenched with the warmth, breath caught in my chest.

"We can sleep in one big puppy pile," Bond murmured, but there was nothing tender and sweet about his tone.

It was filled with hunger, and need, as his green eyes blazed with desire. The bathroom light flicked on and Nero stood in the doorway. "You can take first shower if you want?"

Holy Hell. How was I supposed to be naked in there with three ravenous male Wolves out here?

I swallowed hard as Judas pulled my hand away, and held it in his own. "I told you once before, you don't have to be afraid of us. We'd never do anything you didn't want to do. Go ahead." He motioned to the bathroom. "No one's coming through that door if you don't want them to."

"We'll protect you," Bond growled. "From Poltergeist or weird roommates, or anything else for that matter."

They would. They'd protect me as long as they drew

breath, and that tremor in my chest turned into a heavy thud...*boom boom...boom boom*...I cupped my hand against Bond's cheek. "Thank you. I...*I ah..." love you.* Those words felt natural...felt *real.* I wanted to say them...to Judas, and Nero, and Bond. "You all mean a great deal to me. I want you to know that."

"That's good," Judas murmured. "Because you mean a great deal to us."

Nero nodded, as did Bond.

"Now, you use all the hot water and we're going to have to get warm some other way." Nero smiled, and gave me a wink. "Just sayin'."

I shook my head and dropped Judas' hand before I scooted to the edge of the bed. "Bond looks like he gives great cuddles, I'm sure he won't mind being the big spoon."

"Hold up." Nero jerked his hand in the air and turned a panicked gaze to Bond.

"Yeah." The big guy smiled and rubbed his hands together. "I'll be the big spoon for you, Nero, no worries about that at all."

Judas shoved from the bed and chuckled before motioning to the bathroom. "Go, it's all yours. Use whatever you need."

I grabbed my bag and pajamas and left the Wolves behind. Muffled speaking came from the room before a *thump* came from behind me and they were at it again. Something hard hit the wall. It could've been Nero's head or Bond's butt. But the sound made me smile as I closed the door and looked at Judas' bathroom.

Judas' bathroom was clean and neat, folded towels in a corner. A pair of clean sweat pants and a t-shirt on top of a smaller dresser. I placed my clothes next to his and touched the soft cotton of his shirt. It felt so different from my bathroom, even though I knew they were exactly the same.

I grasped his shirt and lifted it to my nose as another *thud* came from the bedroom.

"You're gonna put his head through the wall in a minute," Judas snapped.

I breathed in the scent of pine, dirt, and freedom before placing his clothing back down. It was nice here, and in this moment, I understood why Ava had ditched me for Chuck. It was good to be wanted, to be taken care of and in return take care of someone. This *connection* I shared with the Wolves was deeper than lust. It was comfort, it was warmth and tenderness. It was *sharing*. I smiled, yanked my skirt down, and then unbuttoned my blouse.

I felt safe here, safer than my own room right now. I dropped my clothes into a pile, strode to the shower and hit the taps. The battle was silent outside the bathroom as I stepped inside carrying my soap and shampoo with me.

I relaxed and closed my eyes, using as much of the hot water as I could.

*A great big puppy pile.* I smiled and scrubbed at the thought, until my skin glowed red with the heat and the room was white with steam. I ended the spray and stepped out.

The bedroom was still quiet, barely even a murmur. I didn't need to have x-ray vision to know all three were staring at the closed door like they could burn holes through the damn thing. I used Judas' towel, buffed my body dry and yanked a comb through my wet hair, before I stared at my pajamas, and then Judas' sweats. My lips curled into a cheeky smile as I made for the basin, and turned on the tap. One swipe of my clothes and they were drenched. "Whoops."

I couldn't possibly wear them now. I turned to that super soft shirt and yanked it over my head before pulling on his cut-off sweatpants and yanking the string taut. I tugged open the door and met each gaze, sparkling with excitement. "Accidently wet my pajamas. I hope it was okay I borrowed these." I plucked at Judas' shirt.

The Alpha's eyes widened. There was a whimper, or it could've been a moan.

Neither Nero or Bond answered, only swallowed hard as their gaze drifted down the clothes.

"I can take them off, if you want?" I murmured.

"What?" Judas jerked his gaze high, his voice husky and raw. "No...*no, that's all good.*"

I glanced at the bed. "Do you guys normally share a bed?"

"No," Judas answered.

"Yes," Nero barked at the same time.

"Every night." Bond nodded.

I just laughed and turned around, sitting on the edge of the bed. "I guess I'll just wait for you guys to shower then."

Nero and Bond looked at each other and then lunged for the doorway at the same time. There was more jostling, and shoving as the two Wolves charged out, slamming the door behind them.

"You know, they don't have to sleep here." Judas took a step closer and reached down to curl his finger around the tip of my chin.

He lifted my gaze, meeting deep brown eyes, the color of honey and earth all mixed into one. "I thought you share everything?"

There was a flare of jealousy before it was smothered once more. A soft bark of laughter was followed by a shake of his head, and he dropped his hand, turning to yank open his cupboard and grab a fresh set of sweats.

"You might regret those words." He stepped into the steam of the bathroom. "But you might regret using all the hot water even more."

A shudder raced through me as he closed the door. It was my turn to stare at the wood as my mind played tricks, taking me back to Thorin, and his forced displays of affection.

He'd kissed me once, and I'd kissed him back. But I didn't know what it felt like to be cared for, to be wanted, and not just because of my father. I didn't know what it was for someone to want me.

The shower turned on with a hiss, as someone from outside called out. *"Lights out!"*

I guess Wolves would wrestle and muck around all night if they were allowed. It was so different from the quiet, almost empty feeling of my own dorm.

I flinched as the door opened and in came Nero, wearing boxers and a tank top. He glanced at the bathroom and then closed the door. "You okay?"

I nodded, pushing backwards and shoving down the bedsheets. "More than okay."

The shower ended as Bond opened the door and came inside, hitting the switch for the overhead lights, plunging the room into darkness. The thin strip of light from under the bathroom door hugged their outlines as the bottom of the bed dipped under their weight.

"Might be a bit of a squeeze," I murmured.

"I don't mind, if you don't." Nero brushed his hand along my leg.

I flinched as the bathroom door opened, and light

flooded the room. Wet hair was tousled, and slick. "Bathroom light on, or off?"

"On," Bond answered, and looked to me for guidance that I'd want the lights off.

I nodded, slipping under the covers in the middle of the bed; Nero did the same beside me.

The bed was bigger than mine, at least a double, and as Judas climbed in next to me and turned on his side to face me, it left plenty of room for Bond to scoot behind Nero as we jostled and shifted.

"You comfortable?" Nero brushed his fingers down my cheek.

"Yeah, I'm good." I smiled. "You?"

"Yeah." He shifted, bumping against my leg.

I swore I heard a clock ticking somewhere in the room, it was so damn awkward. I stared at the ceiling and sighed.

"Hey." Judas shifted against me, making sure to angle his hips away. "Just relax. We're here to protect you, not make you feel awkward."

I smiled at the sound of that, remembering his words from before, and slowly the tension in me eased.

"Better?" He curled his hand around my arm and leaned in, brushing his lips over the t-shirt on my shoulder.

Nero's arm slipped across my stomach as he closed his eyes. We just lay there, as the cool sheets warmed, and that flush from the hot water returned. Judas' finger stroked the inside of my arm, soft and gentle. Putting me at ease.

They all were. Slow steady breaths, the heavy thud of their pulse mingling into one, and the more I focused on their touch, and their smell and their sounds, the more desire flared through me.

Judas opened his eyes at the same time as I did, and

gently pushed up on the bed. The kiss was soft and light, just a brush of his lips.

Hands touched me skimming around my stomach, never straying too far. Fingers entwined with mine. I gripped them tight, feeling Bond's wide hand in mine. I opened my mouth and Judas deepened the kiss.

As he broke away, dark eyes shining, I realized that everything they had hinted at was true. They shared, shared touching, shared kissing. And I liked it.

I turned my head to Nero, meeting the ice blue in his eyes. They shared love. I closed my eyes as Nero kissed me and fully turned towards him.

Judas was at my back, tugging the neckline of my shirt down to kiss the top of my shoulder. Desire flooded through me, filling my ears with the heavy thud of my own heart. I broke the kiss, leaning my head backwards, my hand reaching up to slide my fingers through Judas' damp hair.

Nero brushed his hand past my breast, making me tremble. He lowered his head, kissing a long line down my neck to my collar bone, until with one powerful motion he cupped my breast.

A moan tore free, breathless, weightless.

Just like me.

"Is this okay?" Judas' words were warm against my ear.

I nodded...and then realized it was useless to fight my desires. "Yes."

Bond's hand left mine as the bedsheets shifted. The bedsprings howled, as he kissed the inside of my knee and gently moved upwards. I couldn't track their hands, and their touch. My mind raced as fingers brushed my nipple, and the heat of a breath followed.

"Not too much," Judas commanded.

A tremor tore free, shuddering, jarring, making me arch

my back as Nero's lips closed over the taut peak under his fingers, lips kissed on the outside of Judas' shirt. Fire licked between my thighs, and energy hummed, deeper than I'd ever felt before.

I opened my thighs, letting Bond press his weight down. I wanted them. I wanted this. I wanted to be touched and to touch them. I reached behind me, skimming Judas' hip.

"It's okay," he whispered in my ear, "tonight is all about you."

Bond's hips drove against mine, with a slow thrust.

"More." I trembled. "I want more."

Bond's length grew hard beneath his boxers, pressing against the juncture of my thighs, sending tiny sparks at the edge of my sex. I spread my thighs as Nero's mouth widened, drawing my nipple deeper.

"We're going to take care of you." Judas' words urgent against my ear. "We're gonna take such good care of you."

And those tremors turned urgent with every slow thrust, until I clenched my ass, driving my hips to meet him. He was hard, and ready, and I was so warm and slick. Clothing...I wanted to get rid of the clothing.

My hand left Judas' hip to push down the edge of his sweat pants, but Judas' caught my desperation, slipping his fingers between mine, holding me tightly.

"Soon," he hummed against my neck. "Soon we're going to take turns making you ours...forever."

I couldn't hold on. I couldn't fight it. I couldn't claim it. My hips shot off the bed, thumping against the hard outline of Bond's need. He held it there, lowering his head while he slipped a hand under my body to grasp my ass. He held me hard against him, as his body pulsed against mine.

Blond hair slipped to fall over his eyes as he let a low grunt free.

But I was lifting my leg, curling it around his, trapping him against my throbbing need as I fisted the sheets and let out a cry.

"That's it," Judas urged. "That's where you need to be."

My limbs stopped working, words wouldn't come as I collapsed back against the mattress and Nero slowly lifted his head.

The t-shirt was wet with his mouth, sticking against my skin. Bond collapsed against me, curling at the bottom of the bed. I closed my eyes as tiny shudders tore free, buzzing and humming through my bones.

Hard, heavy breaths took their time to slow. We were quiet, peaceful...*surrendered.*

Hands grasped mine. Bond slid his fingers along the outside of my thigh.

And we lay like that, until sleep moved in like a silent predator.

Stealing me away, as I curled between my three...perfect...*Wolves.*

# CHAPTER FIVE

## DON'T LOOK SO SMUG

"Morning."

I cracked open my eyes to see Judas smile. There was an arm draped around my middle, and someone gripped one of my legs in an embrace. It took me a second to remember where I was, while Judas rose up, propping his head on his hand and watched me.

*The shower...*

I glanced down...*his clothes.*

Memories came flooding back, but they weren't the only thing. A flicker of desire flared between my thighs, and as I breathed their scent the need grew bolder.

Nero opened his eyes and moved his hand against my belly. The only one who was still asleep was Bond, clutching my leg in a stranglehold of an embrace as he let out a snore.

"You should be grateful," Judas murmured. "That snore is all he does."

The nasally honk stilled, before a sudden inhale. "I heard that," the Beta mumbled and leaned closer, pressing his lips to my knee before he rolled away.

"Sleep well?" Nero murmured.

Heat flared through my cheeks as I nodded, "Yes, and you?"

"Very well indeed." He rolled into his back, drawing his hand away as he stretched. "Although, today is going to be Hell."

He shoved up from the bed, half tumbling until perfect reflexes caught his fall. "Because I'll be wishing the day away until it's bedtime again."

Judas chuckled and rolled the other way, leaving Bond to brush his fingers down my shin.

"What makes you think I'm staying tonight?"

There was no answer, just a chuckle before he turned. His erection punched out the front of his boxers, stiff and demanding. I couldn't tear my gaze away.

"Just an inkling I have," he answered.

"Me too," Judas added.

I glanced to him, and *bam!* There he was, thick and hard, the soft fabric of his sweats hugging the outline.

"And me," Bond growled, and shoved from the bed to stand.

My mouth turned arid. Breath stopped. The whole world faded. He was big...like *big.* I remembered the feel of him, pressed against the juncture of my thighs, thick and hard.

"What, no comeback?" Judas chuckled. "Got nothing to say?"

I lifted my gaze, meeting his and gave him the only two words I could. "I'm staying."

"Yeah you are." Bond nodded and strode toward the door.

Nero followed. "And you'll be wishing the day away like the rest of us. Don't think we're going easy on you every night, either. You can't hide under Judas' sweats forever."

*Oh, Hell...*fever raced between my thighs, making me tremble.

*Making me quake.*

"You want to shower?" Judas motioned to the bathroom.

I shoved up from the bed, unable to hide the burning in my cheeks. Nero and Bond left, closing the door behind them, and as much as I'd love to stay here cocooned in the fantasy of my three *gorgeous* Wolves, I couldn't hide here forever. "No, I think I'll head back to my room. Is it okay if I wear these?"

I plucked at the shirt as Judas smiled. "Go ahead, but make sure you don't wash them. In fact, no one is allowed to wash them. I want to be smelling you all over them for the rest of my damn life."

He turned and stepped into the bathroom, not even bothering to close the door before he yanked the shirt over his head and dropped his boxers.

I followed him in, staring at his firm ass clenching as he walked. I grabbed my sodden pajamas and bag of toiletries before I raced for the door.

*"Hey!"* Judas called out. "Don't you want to stay and wash my back?"

His laughter haunted me as I hurried from his bedroom, scanned the foyer and then bolted for the door. The sun was peeking over the horizon. It was early, far too early for me. But for some strange reason I felt fresher than ever.

*Yeah, I wonder why that is.* My own snark echoed.

I hurried, bouncing across the Academy grounds, and reached my own dorm.

The doors scraped, and I winced at the sound. Everything was quiet. They obviously hadn't needed anyone during the night. I gripped the bannister and raced up the stairs, before glancing at Ava's door. Darkness waited inside. She was an early riser, if she was inside, I'd hear her by now, singing...or swearing.

I shoved the key into the door lock and felt dread press in. But when I pushed the door open I saw my roommate standing just inside, still fully clothed. Her mattress still bare, like she hadn't slept at all.

"Look, before you run in and run out, trying your best to avoid me, I just want to let you know, I'm leaving. Moving my bed back down to the basement."

Guilt tore through me as I closed the door and looked at her...like really looked at her tired eyes, the shadows under her eyes, the paleness of her skin. "I'm sorry if I made you feel that way."

"Well, it was a little obvious. It's hard being the new kid. I'm sure you remember what that feels like."

I swallowed hard and dropped my hands. I'd been a bitch to her, a real bitch and it just hit me. "I shouldn't have left you like that."

She gave a little shake and then shifted her stance. "I get it. I'm not angry, just...a little upset. You never knew it, but the thing is, I've been here for a long time." She looked around the room. "Just not in this room."

"Why?" I headed for my cupboard, stowed my bag and draped my wet pajamas over the end of the open door. "Why are you here, and why've you been in the basement this entire time?"

Confusion crowded her gaze. "I wish I knew...I wish I could remember. All I know was two nights ago these things snapped." She lifted her hands, the broken links still dangling from the ends. "And I could move, so I crawled out from the basement, and up here." She turned her head.

"That was my bed in nineteen eighty three, when I came here."

"Do you remember anything, your Mom...your Dad?"

She just shook her head. "Ward of the state."

"There must be something you remember?"

"I remember, feeling cold and drained. Like I could barely move. I tried to wake up for class, tried to get it together. They used to hurt me here." She looked around the room. "Used to lock me in my room, make me miss my class, and I'd have detention. Bestias...hasn't always been a nice place. Not like it is now. It used to be filled with kids who were mean...kids like Brutus."

"Brutus?" I glanced at her. "Who's he?"

She just shook her head. "I don't want to talk about it. Can we please not talk about it?"

"Sure," I murmured. "I'm Mor by the way. Morwenna, but most call me just Mor."

"Hi Just Mor, I'm Cassidy."

"What kind of immortal are you, are you anyway?"

"A shifter," she murmured and looked away. "Of the feathered kind."

"Oh wow." I was in awe. "An eagle? Maybe a hawk...or are you one of those hunting owls?"

"A Flamingo actually." She pulled her foot up, balancing on the inside of her other knee.

"A Flamingo?" I stared until my eyes watered.

"Flamingos can be deadly as fuck," she answered with a cold stare.

I turned away, and stumbled toward the bathroom. "I'm sure they can be. Just gonna take a quick shower and we can continue talking if you want."

But instead of showering I just closed the bedroom door

and wrapped my arms around my middle. "Flamingo?" I whispered before a smile consumed me.

My belly shuddered with laughter, until the tears flowed and I had to slap my hand over my mouth to stifle the sound.

I sat there for a while, laughing and crying, and eventually swiped the tears away and removed Judas' sweats. I hurried, stepping into the shower and washing before I was out, drying myself and yanking open the door. "If you want, we can go down to the basement together—"

I stepped out of the bathroom with the words dying on the tip of my tongue. She was gone...really gone. "Strange girl indeed." I yanked open my dresser and shimmied into fresh panties before turning and yanking on my bra. I had a clean shirt and blouse on before I heard the shower hiss next door, and Ava belting out some kind of tortured Kraken call...or maybe it was her singing.

Anyway, it was good to hear her back. I bounded to the bed, yanked on socks and shoes before brushing my hair. A brush of my lip gloss and I grabbed my bag and headed out the door, ready to spill the news and tell her *everything*.

But I thought about that for a second. Maybe the Wolves didn't want anyone to know. Maybe *I* didn't want anyone to know?

Ava wasn't just anyone though, was she? She was my best friend. My kickass confidante. I inhaled hard and smiled. Maybe I could tell her a little, but just be a little fuzzy on the details.

I shoved her spare key into her lock and stepped inside as she switched off the shower.

"About time you came home...doing the walk of shame, I see."

There was a second, before the bathroom door was

yanked open and my best friend grinned ear to ear. "It's going to be a beautiful day." She gushed and then stepped inside the bathroom to pull her underwear on.

"Sounds like you had a good night."

*"Only the best night ever."*

"So how much would you hate me if I asked you to come down to the basement with me?"

She stilled, and then poked her head out of the doorway. "Why in the world would you want to go down there?"

"Because Cassidy was down there, and she doesn't remember why."

"Cassidy? Who the hell is Cassidy?" She just shook her head and stilled, counted to three under her breath, cowered and yanked open her cupboard door.

"What are you doing?"

"Um, in case you forgot, two bunnies had a fuck fest on my sneakers," she snapped and lunged forward, whipping her hands along the bottom of her hanging clothes before staring into the darkness.

"Anyway," I continued. "She doesn't remember, only about some asshole called Brutus who bullied her."

"He sounds like an asshole." She yanked a blouse from a hanger and then a skirt. "I still don't get why we need to go back down there, not after...you know."

"Because." The words stilled on my lips. *Because I'm responsible.*

"No." Ava yanked up her skirt, fastened the button and turned toward me. "We are not doing this again."

"What?"

"Don't *what* me. I know exactly what you're thinking." She stepped forward and lifted her hands, holding my shoulders and looking me in the eyes. "Not everything that happens because of those things that were done to you is your fault. I want you to understand that. You don't have to shoulder all the burden all the time."

"I wasn't going to —"

"Bullshit. You can lie to everyone else, including yourself, but you can't lie to me Morwenna Livingstone. I know you too well."

I inhaled hard and then exhaled. "I think after this Academy thing is done, I'm going to have to take you out."

"Oh goody, where are you thinking?" She smiled.

"No, I mean, take you out. You know me too well, Ava Blaine. You know all my secrets, my make-up routine, where I stash my by best erasers...everything."

She just rolled her eyes and giggled, before dropping her hands.

"I'm deadly serious."

That just seemed to make her laugh even harder.

"No, for real. I think that if I could somehow understand what happened to her, I could help her a little."

"Like you helped me, you mean?" She cut me a glance with one raised brow.

"We helped each other. I've been mean to her, ignoring her. Not wanting her to be there, and I feel bad."

"Well, okay then. Let's go down and see if we can help her find the asshole that put her down there."

Just like that she was all in. I wrapped my arms around her and pulled her close. "I love you, you know that right?"

She hugged me back, turning her head to rest it on my shoulder. "I know that. I love you too."

Then she pulled away, giving me a smile, and sat on the end of the bed to pull on her socks and shoes. In a second, we were out the door, but instead of heading for the stairs we turned toward the basement door.

Whoever said that Vampires weren't a bunch of

cowards had obviously never met me. I swallowed hard as that haunting sound of scratching resurfaced in my head.

*Scratch...scratch...scratch...scratch...*

Ava just stared at the door beside me.

"Maybe we should come back with reinforcements?"

"Sounds good to me," she answered with a rush, and then spun on the spot and lunged for the stairs.

I raced after her, with my heart hammering and tore down the stairs and through the foyer door.

# CHAPTER SIX

## EVIL LIKE THE OMEN MOVIE

A CRACK OF THUNDER RUMBLED OVERHEAD, SHAKING the ground, and black clouds marred the skies. I hurried my steps across the lawn, other students doing the same, heading for class. The sweet scent of the coming rain sat on the tip of my tongue, any second now...and it'd be teeming.

"What a crap start to the day," Ava murmured. "If I didn't have a pervert poltergeist in my room, I'd stay in bed all day watching movies."

"Have you seen him again?"

"No," she growled and folded her arms tighter across her body. "But he's seen plenty of me."

"As if you'd stay in your room anyway," I teased and nudged her with my shoulder. "You'd be at Chuck's place."

Her cheeks blushed, and it made me laugh that she still felt so embarrassed about her and Chuck. I mean, sure, it was a little strange. But only because I grew up with him and he was family, but love didn't always play by the rules. When you fell, you dropped like a brick to the bottom of the ocean in love.

My three Wolves came to mind... *love*, I'd had this thought before, but I struggled to say it then, just as I struggled now. Still the feeling hummed inside me. We'd definitely grown closer. In fact, one tiny slip of clothing was all that stood in our way.

I was lost to the memory of Bond. Maybe that was love... I think it was love. Giddiness swirled in my gut like dozens of butterflies. Yep, whatever I felt was damn real.

A heavy sigh bought me from the memory. Ava was smiling, trying her best to keep burning redness from swallowing her entire face.

"Hey, no more blushing," I teased. "You like him, go be with him."

"I just can't stay away. All those muscles, those hands." She lifted her own. "When he kisses me, his—"

"Nope. No way. That's the line crossed. No talking about bedroom antics or smooches. Deal?"

She cut me a glare, but I just couldn't picture Chuck as anything but a guard.

"Deal." She nodded. "And no wild stories about your Wolves." She giggled, her expression softening.

She pushed the strap of her bag over her shoulder. The thing was gigantic and I hadn't seen her use it before. "Um, what's going on? You carrying around a second wardrobe?" The bag suddenly moved and shifted, and I inspected it closely. "What the hell have you got in there?"

Sighing, she swung the bag forward and pried it open.

A small animal head popped out, grey fur grizzled with black. My badger made bird-like coos, glancing from me to Ava.

"Why do you have Jubba in your bag?" I reached down and scratched his head, fingering the cherry red ribbon around his neck. "He's a *he*." I tugged at the ribbon, but Ava swung her bag out of my reach.

"Boys like ribbons too and he looks cute. Plus, with me staying at Chuck's more often, Jubba and I have bonded. He doesn't attack my clothes, and he follows me around...*everywhere*."

"I think it's adorable." I smiled, wanting to be the one to look after him. But the timing just never seemed right.

Jubba ducked his head back in, and Ava looked down at him, "Now be a good boy and sleep during class, okay?" She adjusted her bag over her shoulder and together we headed to class.

An inhuman groan sliced through the silence. "B...back to c...class."

We jumped at the same time, spun to see Principal Stone lurch along the lawn, dragging one foot behind,

*Oh shit....*

"Are you seeing this?" A tremor danced in Ava's voice. "We buried her. She was dead."

Principal Stone lifted one dirt crusted arm toward the other students as they stumbled out of her path. Grave dirt and maggots fell, leaving a trail behind her.

"I don't think she's a ghost," I murmured.

"Are we talking zombie?"

I nodded, unable to take my eyes off the teacher, hearing her bones crack as she moved. Seeing the undead, coupled with the dark storm clouds, it felt like the apocalypse neared.

"You think she knows?"

Ava jerked her gaze to mine. "What, that you killed her?"

"Shhh." I lunged closer, slapping my hand over her mouth before I looked around.

Muffled words warmed my palm.

"What?" I jerked my hand away, staring into her eyes.

"What's going on at this school?" Ava grabbed my arm to move as Principal Stone spun, staring at us with cloudy white eyes.

"M...morwenna L...livingstone," she growled.

"Fuck." My skin crawled.

Ava hauled me behind her and we ran, darting across the lawn, along with several other students who were screaming. "She remembers me," I said. "Is she back for revenge? Is she going to tell everyone what happened?"

I looked over my shoulder at Ms. Stone; she approached in a sloppy gait, snapping her jaws open and shut. The skin had peeled away from her arms, and I shivered at the sight.

We dove for the doors of the building and bolted into a hallway with hardly anyone around. Eeriness closed in around us.

"Just don't start freaking out. But I swear if I wake up as a zombie, I'm coming after you first," Ava started.

"Why me?"

A moan came from outside, and we rushed down the hall.

"It's no fun eating brains on my own. Plus, imagine all the humans we can trap with us working as a team. Brains galore for both of us."

"Eww. And I don't think you can turn me since I'm already technically dead."

Ava eyed me. "I'm sure there's a way." The determination was fierce in her, and a tiny bit terrifying.

"But Ava, what if she tells someone I killed her," I whispered.

Ava was shaking her head. "No one's going to believe a zombie."

Her words hung in the air. They felt false. But what other option did I have?

"Help me!" A kid wailed and kicked his legs, which were ten inches off the ground.

Great big globs of green goo stuck him to the row of metal lockers and seemed to criss-cross over his body like a spider's web of muck. He bucked and writhed to free himself while Mr. Maling, our P.E. teacher, had one foot propped up against the locker, his hands gripping the poor guys' arms. He pulled to free him, in what looked like an unwinnable tug-o-war match.

"What the hell?" Ava was hugging her bag with Jubba to her chest.

Someone nudged my back, and I spun around, a scream on my throat, expecting to find Ms. Stone.

But instead, it was Salome and Nesrin. "Shit's gone sideways today." They were staring at the guy caught in goo.

"Get to class," Mr. Maling shouted like this was some everyday occurrence.

And we all rushed on, heading upstairs only to find Judas, Bond and Nero standing in front of the classroom door, reading a note stuck to it.

"Hey babe." Judas' hand slid into mine, our fingers intertwined. And for those few moments, I let myself fall into his dark eyes, remembering our time together, the pleasure my three Wolves awakened within me. Fire ignited in my chest, but this was different. The sensation spread lower inside me, and an inferno was alight between my thighs as fast as sparking a match.

"Gah." Ava nudged Bond aside to reach the door. "We're facing the apocalypse and you're stopping to exchange smoochie glances."

Salome and Nesrin were rolling their eyes.

Nero shifted to my back, his arms wrapped around my stomach, and we all turned to read the sign on the door.

*History class. Today you have a free period for research. Don't squander your time.*

"Fuck, this is bullshit," Bond growled.

"No one said we couldn't all work on a similar historical location," I offered.

"And what's that gonna be," Bond asked, turning away from the door. "The cafeteria, because I'm hungry?"

I shrugged. "Not sure yet. We only just got the assignment."

"Wait a minute," Judas added. "They want anything we researched on history, right? So, we dig up the history of this Academy."

"Love it." Ava turned to Nesrin and Salome. "You two joining us?"

The felines glanced my way as if waiting for my approval, and after what I'd learned about Brylee, about Salome's background, and how danger was on her heels, I wanted to embrace them, help them. We all made mistakes, faced shit in our lives.

So, I nodded. "The more the merrier."

Their smiles made me happy.

"The lodge it is," Judas commanded. "They have a collection of history books on the Academy."

"I can't believe they still want us to work on assignments while the school's flooded in ghosts and zombies," Ava droned, her shoulders dropping.

"Zombies? Where?" Nero's gaze flew left and right along the hallway, his eyes wide and bright as if the notion excited him.

"Ms. Stone is back," I murmured. "She's out the front of the building."

"You sure she's not just a ghost?" Nesrin asked.

"She had maggots falling off her body." Ava waved for us to follow her. "Let's head out the back exit to avoid her. Think she wants to send Mor to detention." She sniggered to herself and pushed her bag strap higher on her shoulder as Jubba wriggled inside.

The lodge was empty and no one else was there, so we locked the door behind us to avoid any surprise zombie interruptions.

Nero and Bond were in the corridor, ordering hot chocolates from the vending machine for everyone, while the rest of us carried every damn mammoth book we could find into the main room and dumped them on the small table between the circle of couches.

"Looks like it's a day of reading." I flopped into the seat, Judas on one side and Ava on the other. Salome grabbed the top leather bound book and crashed onto the opposite couch, her legs crossed under her as she started flicking through.

"Snacks," Nesrin declared. "I know where the teachers keep a collection and this calls for *borrowing* some."

"Yes," Judas called out. "I'm starving. Only had one breakfast this morning." He reclined, his knees wide, brushing against me.

"You know if the world is coming to an end, I wouldn't want to face it with anyone else but you guys." I laid a hand on Judas' thigh and his arm looped around my back.

"Well if that's the case, I don't want to die while doing some lame-ass research on a snorefest history assignment." Ava was digging a hand into her bag and pulled out Jubba, the tiny thing's fur was all ruffled. He made the cutest growling sounds as she settled him on the couch between us, drawing my attention to his toenails.

"You painted them pink?" I reached over and pushed down the messed up hair across his back.

"It's what we do when we hang out." Ava shrugged.

"What's that doing here?" Bond snarled, walking into the room, carrying four cups of hot chocolate before placing them on the table, glaring at Jubba.

The hair on the back of the badger's neck fuzzed, and he snarled at the Wolf.

With everyone back in the room, we all settled down, books in our laps, and started reading.

Several rounds of drinks later and empty chip and chocolate packets all over the place, I pressed my spine into the couch, stretching my back. "I might be going cross-eyed."

Ava was yawning and cuddling Jubba to her chest, kissing his head. Open books lay all over the room with potential ideas for our assignment, but nothing sounded exciting enough.

"I found something," Bond declared loud and proud of himself. "That old church on the grounds is fucking evil."

"Evil like the Omen movie, or just assholes who hide dirty secrets in their basements?" Nero quizzed, clapping shut his book, throwing up a small plume of dust into the air.

Bond rose up from the desk, carrying the open book with him. "Apparently, a psychotic emotional Vampire student called Brutus went to this school. But he wasn't content with just stealing souls. The sick sonofabitch wanted to take their immortal lives too. He butchered over fifty people. Students, teachers, but mostly anyone he hunted outside school grounds. And the creepy part? All those bodies are buried right here, at Bestias Academy...and by the looks of all these missing pages, I'd say someone wanted to cover this up."

"Holy shit," Ava snorted. "So are all these ghosts around the school his victims? Why the hell are they all roaming the school now?"

Everyone shrugged.

"Well, I vote we research the church." I lifted my hand, and slowly, one by one everyone did the same, including Jubba with Ava's help.

"Hell, that's creepy history," Bond muttered. "And it's right here at our school."

A silence fell over us, and all I imagined was being at the Academy at that time, attending class with a serial killer.

*Bang. Bang. Bang.*

We all jumped in our seats, staring toward the window. A hulking form hovered there, glaring at us, shrouded in the shadows of the trees crowding the window.

Nesrin let out a small squeak, and Judas pushed me behind him as he rose to his feet.

*Bang.* "Ava, let me in!" his muffled voice cried out.

I peered past Judas as Ava climbed to her feet. "Chuck? Is that you?"

"Yes!" The figure moved from the window, and Ava darted to the front door.

"Fuck, I almost peed my pants." Salome collapsed back into her seat. And suddenly everyone broke out into a nervous laughter at how quickly we'd all jumped.

"So, we still want to go visit the church?" I asked.

Judas scoffed. "I want to see the cemetery first, maybe the gravestones will give us something more to go on. But yeah, nothing scares me."

Bond tapped his chest twice with a closed fist. "I'm ready."

Nero unleashed a loud howl and shook himself.

All right, we were headed back to the cemetery where I'd buried Principal Stone, and then the damn church where I almost lost my life.

# CHAPTER SEVEN

## THE DESTROYER OF SOUPS

THE MOUND OF FRESH DIRT WAS PILED HIGH IN THE cemetery, as though the earth had expelled Principal Stone for being the hideous, uncontrollable bitch she had been. To our right was the church, but too many memories waited for me there.

The horror...

And the pain.

"Jeez." Bond stared at the trampled mess and winced. "Grave dirt everywhere."

"Don't tell me a big, bad Wolf like you is afraid of a little mud?" Ava muttered and stared at the same pile we all did.

Still the lovable goofball rose to the bait. "I'm not afraid."

"Go on then." Ava motioned with her head. "Go in there."

Brittle old posts criss-crossed together to circle the cemetery. Some of them had fallen down, although I wondered why there were any to begin with. Spells were the only thing keeping the dead from the living, and by living, I meant those like me as well. But what happened the night of the Witch storm had somehow cancelled out all the power these incantations once had.

And now there were ghouls and spirits walking the grounds where they were murdered. *One by me.* I stiffened with the memory, and swallowed the bitter tang of acid in the back of my throat as Bond took a step forward, the toe of his boots hovering over the demarcation on the ground.

"I'll go," I said and stepped forward, turning my hand to brush his fingers with mine.

This was my Witch storm and this was my Zombie arisen.

"Mor, I didn't mean…" Ava murmured and stepped with me.

But I wanted to know the deep and dark secrets that Bestias Academy hid from us, and I wanted to put the tortured souls to rest, once and for all. "It's okay." I skirted the pile of dirt and glanced at the derelict building.

The church looked even more rundown than I remembered. I hated everything about it. The lofty, pointed roof, the shattered, dirty windows. Even the smell…from out here, everything smelled.

Judas kicked a mound of dirt before staring at the front door and climbed the step to the porch. My thoughts were foggy, nerves jumpy as Hell. I twisted the ring on my finger, around and around, remembering the pain and the terror.

The felines had hurt me in there…stole my ring, left me to blister and die from the sun.

And I would have, if not for Ava and the Wolves.

Nesrin's arm brushed against mine as she joined me in staring at the church. "If I could take back what we did, I'd do it in a heartbeat."

Salome stepped up on my other side. "I hate this place."

"Can't agree more," I murmured. "And Brylee was

behind it all..." I snarled. "Her and that piece of shit Thorin. I hope he's dead. I hope he gets exactly what's coming to him."

Nesrin stepped closer, and I froze at first, but she wrapped her arms around my shoulders and hugged me, and I swore I heard her sniffle. Salome joined our hug, and there was something warm and satisfying about feeling their regret.

Ava was there in seconds, throwing herself into the hug, and we all broke out laughing.

"Is this a communal hug fest, and can anyone jump in?" Chuck mocked.

"You get free hugs when you want, Big Guy," I said, while Ava looped her arms around his middle.

"I have endless hugs for you." And they looked at each other with such devotion. I'd never seen Chuck this way in all the years we grew up together, and the happiness suited him. Better than his broody, dark warrior personality.

"You think Jubba will be okay in the lodge bedroom?" she asked Chuck.

He pushed a strand of hair behind her ear. "He'll be fine. He's got an entire bed to shred to pieces. It'll keep him occupied for a whole minute at least."

Nero stepped closer to me, his hand sliding into mine. "Want to look around?"

No one answered, it wasn't a *yay, let's do this,* kind of moment.

Still Nesrin and Salome muttered, and stepped forward studying the headstones. Ava had her phone out, snapping photos of the location, which was perfect for our assignment.

Nero drew me closer and we scanned the names.

*Arthur Acton*

*July 12, 1941*
*Died*
*May 11, 1968*

"He's young." I kneeled and tried to read the dedication but it was too worn from the weather.

I moved to the next gravestone and another to find most of them perished within a few years of each other.

"Don't think the bodies are buried here," Judas called out from across the yard. "Surely their families wanted them close to home if they were killed on campus."

Made sense. "So why are there so many ghosts still on the grounds?"

"Maybe not all the bodies were found?" Chuck suggested.

I flinched at the words and my new roommate, Cassidy, filled my head. She said she wasn't a ghost, and yet she seemed pretty well haunted.

"Maybe there were other deaths after that incident." Ava stared out toward the woods to where we'd buried Principal Stone.

Behind Judas, a faint fog rolled in from the surrounding woods, crawling forward like a disease to infect this place.

"I think we should get inside now." Ava stared at the fog and then turned toward the building.

But I was more afraid of the church than I ever was of the white mist creeping toward us. Heavy footsteps echoed, and the howling creak of floorboards cut through the air. Chuck reached his side and dragged out a dagger from his hip.

He wasn't going in alone. Judas climbed the stairs behind him, Nero and Bond close behind, and through the shattered windows, a soft neon green light swelled.

"Umm, guys." Ava stared as the light inside grew. "There's something in there."

Judas stilled at the edge of the porch as the light grew brighter inside.

*Morwenna.*

I flinched at the ghostly whisper of my name and whipped my head toward the ghostly mist reaching through the cemetery grounds. "Oh Hell no, not again."

Ava flinched and scurried as fast as I moved to mount the steps behind the Wolves.

"Move it or lose it," she snapped, barrelling into Bond, and then Chuck, before she reached for the already half open door.

I was racing behind her as that low, pain-filled moan came from the fog once more. *Mooorrrrwwweeennnnaa...*

Ava punched the door, flinging it against the wall with a *bang.* And that green glow pulsed brighter.

"Who the fuck comes here?" The savage snarl came from inside the building.

I glanced past the fallen pews to the walkway where I crawled for my damn life months before. The Wolves, Chuck and Nesrin and Salome crowded in behind us.

"Who the fuck is asking?" Nesrin snarled and took a step forward. Dark eyes flashed with anger, but a sneer followed, full of sass.

The green glow shimmered with the stench of a thousand years.

"Oh jeez," Nero snapped. "Bond?"

"*That* wasn't me," the Wolf growled.

But the shimmering glow darkened into the outline of a man...*a very big man.* Between the pews he strode, wearing a bomber jacket about ten sizes too small. The sleeves rode halfway up his arms, the seams split. Jowls draped around his face, dividing my focus from the beady black inhuman eyes.

*"I'm Brutus, Destroyer of Souls!"* The apparition roared as he stumbled toward us.

"Brutus?" Bond hissed and cut a panicked glance my way. "From the book in the lodge."

I flinched with the connection as the apparition squeezed between the pews, to shoot out of the end with a *plop*.

"Destroyer of Souls?" Ava winced at him. "More like Destroyer of Soups." She lifted a hand, pointing to some ugly brown stain on the front of his shirt. "Ah, buddy, you got a bit of shit right there." Her throat tightened before she retched at the sight.

He looked down at the smear of last centuries' gravy and plucked at his shirt, lifting it to his nose before he sniffed and tried to lick it.

"That's just nasty," Chuck growled, unable to take his gaze off the foul spirit.

And those dark beady eyes focused on us once more. But it wasn't just the grub of a ghost I was interested in, it was the green glow that seemed to reach up through the floorboards. The glow grew brighter through the cracked and broken parts. I lifted a hand, and pointed. "Guys, there's something down there."

But Brutus Destroyer of Soups wasn't sharing the attention with anyone. And with a piercing roar he took two heaving strides, and then lunged through the air.

Power ripped from the center of my chest, as though the Dragon's Tear was still wedged inside. I threw up my hands, protecting my face as Chuck swung his dagger and charged forward, meeting the messy spirit head on.

But as he connected, the foul creature seemed to disappear. Laughter rippled out in the church around us.

*You thought,* the spirit snarled. *You could get rid of me that easy...not now that I've returned.*

I spun, scanning the darkened corners and the pews.

Judas strode forward, Nero and Bond alongside him, before they turned. "He's gone."

"Not gone," Nesrin snarled. "He's playing with us."

Still the rippling green light beckoned as I motioned toward the broken floor. "I don't care about him. I want to know what's down there."

# CHAPTER EIGHT

## BUT...

"You sure you want to go down there?" Ava turned toward me, looking sickly in the green glow. "We don't even know what's down there."

"Can't be any worse than him, can it?" Nesrin stared at the open church door as movement came from outside.

There was a *crash* and then a "Fuck!" from Brutus, before Nesrin shook her head.

"A ghost with a mouth, great. Like we need someone else with an attitude around here." She glanced at the broken floorboards and took a step, standing at the edge and looking down. "I'll go."

"We don't know what's down there," Judas murmured.

"It's for a project, right?" She lifted her head. "So we research the hell out of it. Besides, when did you turn into a wimp?"

She glanced my way and shook her head, and that old Nesrin was back in a heartbeat...making the fire in me lash out. "He's not a *wimp*." I snarled and stepped closer. "You want to go down there so badly." I motioned with my hand. "Go right ahead.'

There was a spark of fear in her eyes, before she swallowed hard and turned to the cracked floorboard.

Salome stepped closer and knelt, tracking her fingers along the crack in the floor. "There's a latch here." She worked a metal hook from between two boards and yanked.

The section of the floor swung up with a groan and a plume of green smoke seemed to rise from the bowels of whatever was down there.

Salome lifted her head to Nesrin, and then me. "I'll go first."

"Don't be silly," the Panther snarled beside her. "I'll go."

She balanced on one leg and stepped down into the hole.

I moved closer, craning my head to see a ladder bolted to the side of the hole. "Nesrin."

She flinched and jerked her gaze to me, terror welling in her dark eyes. "What?"

"Nothing, just...be careful."

There was a curl of her lips before she grabbed the first rung with her hand. "Thanks for the pep-talk, Livingstone. You really helped me out there."

She was gone, sinking into that hole in the middle of the church floor until all I could see was top of her head, and then she jumped, landing with a *thud*.

"You can come down, Salome," she called.

The Lioness was next, sinking into the green pit of foulness with one foot and then another. I stepped closer, reaching one foot out.

"No, Morwenna. Let me go first." I glanced up to Chuck, as he shucked off his jacket, and unbuttoned the cuffs of his perfectly pressed white shirt, before rolling the sleeves along thick, corded muscles.

He was my guard first, always, before my friend. Those

cold, unflinching eyes told me there was no wiggle room in his command, and Ava just gave a soft, need-filled sigh behind him.

"That's so hot," she murmured, never once taking her eyes from him. "So, *so,* incredibly hot."

Hot or not, he sank to his knees, gripped the side of the ladder with one hand, and heaved his muscled frame through the trap door. With one swift lunge, he hit the bottom with a *boom*.

"Wait there," he commanded Nesrin and Salome, shifting his body to scrape his spine against the dirt wall as not to bump into them.

There wasn't much wiggle room. I gripped the ladder, waiting for him to give the all clear.

"No, Mor." Bond knelt on the other side. I lifted my head, to see desire in his eyes. "Let me go first."

"But..." I stammered.

"Let us do this." Nero dropped to his knees.

"All clear," Chuck called out.

Bond was down the hole in the floor in an instant, and then Nero followed.

"We'll protect you," Judas murmured with a soft smile, and then followed the rest of the Wolves into the darkness.

I just lifted my gaze to Ava. We were the only ones left in the church now. "But." The others slipped away in the dark far below. "I'm stronger than all of them."

She just gave a shrug and screwed up her face. "We both are. Just...let them do what they want to do."

I gave a hard sigh, and with a shake of my head I finally stepped into the green mist that felt cold to the touch. Ava came down after me. Voices drifted to me as I hit the bottom. The ground inclined down. I ducked and stepped onto a ramp that led into a massive cavern.

Chuck lifted his head from amongst piles of metal cabinets. "I can't find where the mist is coming from."

It didn't matter, not at this moment. It filled the room, giving us more than enough light to see what this was.

"It's like a work room." Bond stepped to a desk piled high with rolled papers and an old, broken lamp. "Someone lived down here."

"Someone who knew a great deal about the Academy." Chuck ran his fingers along folders in an open drawer. "There's records here dating back the last three hundred years."

"Some as recent as last month." Judas stared at a pile of folders that looked brand new.

"What?" I gripped the railing and stepped into the massive room.

Every inch was filled with desks and cabinets. Even the dirt walls weren't immune from the sheer volume of information. Maps were stuck on jutting rocks. The outline of the Academy grounds, and even some of the dorms...I stilled on ours, and then turned away.

"They've got files on every breed of immortal here," Chuck murmured. "Ghouls, Demi-Gods, Hellhounds..."

Salome winced. "Any Pride's?"

He yanked the drawer open further, rifled through the folders, and then moved the drawer above it. Metal on metal howled, filling the space with the jarring sound. I winced as he yanked out a folder. "Yes, there is."

Salome turned sideways, making her way through the crammed walk space to get to the cabinet. Chuck stepped away, letting her have all the room she needed.

Papers were shuffled as she flicked through the thick folder. "My dad is here...and my mom." She was quiet for a long time. I stepped up to the desk, pushing aside a stack of papers. "There's two more. One female from the seventeen hundreds, and another. An Arson Arlo."

"Arson Arlo?" Bond murmured. "I think I saw his name in the Book of the Dead."

"Killed on the academy grounds in 1983." She flicked open the page. "Along with a shifter, Cassidy Greyson. He's hot too...super hot."

I stilled at the same. *1983?* "You have an image of her, this Cassidy Greyson?" I surged forward as Salome flicked open the pages and lifted a black and white image. "A few actually. But you don't want to see those. This one."

Salome lifted the image of a fresh-faced, smiling young woman. Even before I reached the cabinet, I knew it was her. She had the same hair-spray coated teased mound on the top of her head, and the same sad, lonely smile. "I know her." I murmured. "She's my new roommate."

"What?" Chuck growled. "You don't have a roommate. Your father made sure of that before you stepped foot in this place."

I rose a brow and turned to him. "So that's why. And I do now...*kinda.* She's a ghost, although she thinks she's still alive. She was killed, in our dorm."

"In the basement," Salome added. "I read up and it seems like our good old friend Brutus here lured her and her best friend, Arson down to the basement, before he chained them up and killed both of them."

"God, that's horrible," Nesrin murmured. And those words echoed around the room. "I want to get out of here." She wrapped her arms around her body.

"Me too." Salome shoved all the images inside the file before she shoved it in the drawer.

"Look at this," Ava called.

There was a grating scrape as she grabbed the hilt of a

sword and heaved it free. The ornate markings along the blade shimmered under the coat of grime. I headed for her, staring at the weapon. "That's gorgeous."

"There's another," she said.

I stilled in front of the rusted metal bucket and the hilt of the other and dragged it free.

"I always wanted a broadsword like this one." My best friend smiled, running her finger alongside the edge.

My heart fluttered as I whispered, "Me too."

"We could train." She beamed.

"I'll train you." Chuck was deadly serious. Dark eyes sparkled as he watched her wielding the weapon.

"Right, grab them and anything else we need for this damn assignment and let's go. I want out of this place," I added.

Nesrin was already climbing the slope to disappear into the gloom. Ava grabbed her sword as the Wolves followed.

"You never cease to surprise me." Judas just stared as I carried the sword and made for the ramp.

"That's a good thing, right?" I answered with a smile.

"A very good thing." He lifted a hand, ruffling my hair before he turned.

We all climbed out of the trap door in the middle of the church. But this time there was no Brutus waiting for us. There was nothing but the glowing green light that spilled out of the trapdoor to fill the church.

I carried the sword, walking beside my best friend as we left the church, and the haunted grounds behind. My thoughts were weighed down with somber thoughts as we headed back to the dorm, until as we grew near Chuck lifted his head and growled. "Wait."

Through the trees I saw the guards. That many guards

wasn't the big deal...but all of them waiting at the entrance to our dorm was.

Chuck stepped forward, shoulders squared, breaking through the treeline first before we all followed.

Hellhounds watched the Vampire bodyguard with all the damn careful respect his presence conjured. One of the guards stepped forward as we neared, he scanned all of us, lingering on the swords in mine and Ava's hands.

"Salome Kinraide? You're wanted in the Principal's office...*immediately.*"

"What for?" Nesrin growled.

But the guard never answered, just looked past us to the Lioness at our back.

"I think I know," Salome responded as she inhaled the air.

We all did the same, dragging the scent of the immortals into our lungs. But there was one heady scent amongst all of them...one that chilled her to the bone as she whispered.

"He's here...my Uncle has found me."

# CHAPTER NINE

## A PROPOSAL LIKE NO OTHER

I jerked my gaze toward her as Salome shook her head and took a step backwards.

"No...no way," Nesrin growled and jerked a panicked gaze at her friend.

Something passed between them, a look of hopelessness...and affection.

The guard stepped forward. "This way."

Desperation bloomed in the golden light of the Lioness' eyes. "I have to go," she murmured and looked to Nesrin. "He'll never give up otherwise. He'll never stop hunting me."

Nesrin lifted a hand, fingertips brushing Salome's hand, and for the first time I saw it...Nesrin *cared*...like *really cared*.

An ache flared across my chest at the sight of her pain. I'd never seen her like this, never so *vulnerable*.

"If you're going, then I am too," Nesrin demanded.

"Me too." I stepped forward, meeting the guard's gaze.

"And me" Ava stepped closer.

"Looks like we're all going," Chuck said with a growl.

There was the shake of a head, as the main guard met every gaze, stilling on mine. I crossed my arms. *Your move.* There was a twitch of a nerve at his temple, before he cut Chuck a glare. "Fine, as long as the Lioness comes, I don't care."

He stepped forward, grasped Salome by the arm, and was met with the savage snarl of Nesrin. His hand fell, landing against his thigh as he nodded toward the main building.

Nesrin and Salome walked in front. Ava, and I tracked after them, with the Wolves and Chuck close behind.

No one said anything, not the guards, or Salome, who glanced over her shoulder as we strode toward the main building, and then inside as a Hellhound held open the door.

Footsteps echoed like gunshots in the hallway until the head guard stilled at Principal Balefire's office. The sickly stench of dread was choking. I swallowed hard as movement came from inside the office. Shadows splashed across the glass before the door jerked open.

Amber flames danced in midnight eyes. He jerked his gaze to Salome and then the rest of us. "What's the meaning of this?"

"You asked for Salome," Nesrin growled, anger flashing in dark eyes as she met the Principal's gaze. "I go where she goes."

There was a twitch of his nose before he slipped outside, shutting the door behind him. "No, not going to happen. There's already too many...too many of your kind. I can't risk it."

Nesrin shook her head, anger turned to pain in an instant. "Please," she whispered.

But there was no give in his decision. Principal Balefire shook his head. "I'm sorry."

Nesrin's lip curled at the answer, there was rage behind her eyes. Deep-seated rage as she turned that gaze to me. "The Vampire, what about her?"

I shook my head. I wasn't the one she needed, or the one she wanted.

A tiny, wounded sound came from Nesrin. She jerked her gaze away, the corner of her eye shining with fresh tears. The sight was a punch to my chest. "I'll do it." I wrenched my gaze to Principal Balefire. "Please, Sir. Let me sit in with Salome."

He shook his head. "What for?"

"Can't you see she's scared? Everyone has a right to support when under duress."

I stretched out my hand for Salome as the Guard stepped closer, reaching for me and earning a savage, rippling snarl from both my Wolves and Chuck.

Balefire just glared. "Leave her. Let them both come."

He turned, shoving open the door, leaving us to follow in his wake. Salome grabbed my hand, glancing at me, before she followed. Fear filled her eyes. Making her squeeze my hand tight.

She wasn't my best friend. I owed her nothing. But in this moment, we were soldiers, walking into battle together. Those kinds of moments stay with you, just as I knew this would stay with me.

I turned my head to see Nesrin place her hands to the frosted glass door as Balefire closed it behind us.

The heady scent of male was overwhelming. I swallowed the air, glancing at a man sitting crossed legged on the other side of Balefire's desk, three more stood behind him. The same sandy colored hair, same...*stench*.

Her uncle lifted his head as we entered, golden eyes skirting across me, before they settled on Salome, and that's where they stayed.

He was older than I'd expected, a hard weathered face with a splattering of freckles and dried lips, but it was his eyes I couldn't look away from. Eyes devoid of any warmth, even though they shone like the sun themselves. He might faintly resemble Salome on the outside, but on the inside, this Lion was rotten to the core.

"I'd prefer to talk to Salome in private," the man in the fancy coat stated, his chin lifted high.

Balefire placed the folder in his hands on the table and turned to the man. "Mr. Kinraide, while Salome is attending my school, she's under my care...*and protection*. So, to answer your demand, no, you won't be permitted to talk with Salome in private." Balefire cut me a look of exhaustion. "Even if I allowed it, I doubt you'd get the chance."

For a second, I thought I saw a flicker of pride.

"Mor stays," Salome demanded and squeezed my hand.

"It's okay," I answered. "I'm not going anywhere."

There was a snarl as the man calling himself kin gripped Balefire's desk and leaned closer. "And what if I told you she was never enrolled at this Academy?"

My heart punched inside my chest. Salome's hand went weak against mine. She was slipping, falling away from me, until I grabbed her tight.

Balefire said nothing, just stared at the Alpha male across his desk before he finally leaned forward and opened a folder filled with records. I caught her name typed across the front. "According to my records, she's enrolled."

But her Uncle stiffened, leaned across the Hellhound's

desk and snatched the records. "She hasn't signed it...and there's no record here of a request ever going to her home."

I glanced at Salome, and then moved fast, ruffling the papers in the desk, and the Lion's hair as I snatched the paperwork back and forced a laugh. "She's so forgetful."

I drove my hand through the air behind me, without shifting my gaze from the lying piece of shit sitting in front of me. "Sign it, Salome. This way we know for sure you're meant to be here."

She grabbed the paper, and the hurried scrawl of a pen across a desk filled the room. "Now that's done."

There was a wince as the Lion stared at me. "That's not why I'm here."

"Then, please." Balefire was losing patience, turning a barely tolerating snarl into something dangerous. "Enlighten us."

"As the true heir to the family bloodline, I'm here to give our kingdom a King. We've been under attack, and it's done nothing but left us weak...and the other prides unstable, and that cannot do. By right of pride law, I'm here to claim what is rightfully mine."

He lifted that soulless gaze to Salome. "We'll marry at dawn, and *you will* return the Chalotite stone to me."

She shook her head as I turned toward her. Her eyes wide, panic creeping into the gold, and a deep guttural growl rolled through her chest. "I'll die before I marry you," she spat.

He shoved from his seat, didn't even look at me, but glared at Salome with daggers. "You dare speak to me with such disrespect? You took from me once...*but you won't again.*"

"I took from you?" Her voice was husky, and raw. "*I took from you?*" Tears glistened and rained down her cheeks. "You killed my father, in cold blood...*and then you killed my mother*. My mother, who never hurt a soul."

"Pack law states..."

*"I DON'T CARE ABOUT PACK LAW!"* she roared, rattling the glass windows...stilling the men in the room.

But I knew what they saw when they looked at her. It was the same thing as men like this saw in me. Just one more woman to control. Just one more to placate.

He pushed to his feet as energy prickled along my flesh. Her uncle inhaled hard, jaw bulging as he stared at her. "I'm giving you the chance to do the right thing. But make no mistake. I won't be returning without both you and the stone."

He moved faster than expected, as did the three Lions at his back, barging me aside to grab her. Chairs howled as they too were shoved aside.

But I caught my balance, surging forward as he grasped her arm. *"No!"*

*"Enough!"* Power crackled through the room.

Male power...dark power...*Hells power*.

Her uncle turned his head to his guards. "Search her room for the stone."

"No, you can't do that." She thrashed in his grip, jerking and turning. But he wouldn't let go.

I whipped my gaze to Balefire, desperation cracked my teeth as I ground my jaw. *Do something!*

"Step a foot outside this office without my consent and you'll be met with *my* force." Balefire glared at Kinraide.

"Dad would never have never given his consent to this," Salome cried, yanking her hand, as tears streamed down her face. "He'd rather die."

Kinraide wrenched his gaze to her. "And that's exactly what he did, didn't he?"

Salome stilled, staring into those eyes filled with the sun. She stopped fighting, stopped, breathing even. "Is that what happened, Uncle?"

Arid lips, smashed together until they were bloodless.

"That's exactly what happened. You went to him, didn't you? You went to him and he forbade it. You had no choice then...hide in my father's shadow...or commit murder."

"I did what had to be done, for the sake of the pride."

I stepped forward, pushing between them and met his glare. "You'll have to kill me too...*or die trying.*"

"Hold the *Hell* on," Balefire snapped. "No one is killing *anyone.*"

"She's a liar and a thief. And this has *nothing* to do with your Academy. Five minutes is all I need, and we'll leave you be. There'll be no more trouble. I give you my word."

Shivers of disgust climbed up my spine, and Salome trembled beside me.

"I said *no.*"

*The* hair on my arms stood on end as Balefire stepped around his desk. The fire in his eyes turned from amber to red in an instant. Muscles of his neck bulged with the curl of his lips. I'd never seen Balefire like this before...not *dangerous.* "This is *not* your school, and these are *not* your students. I have a responsibility to protect these children with all the force I deem necessary. Now, I've given you time to state your claim...and *I will investigate this claim*...in due course."

He leaned across the edge of his desk and picked up the phone, and with one simple command he placed the phone back down.

The door opened, heavy footsteps filled my ears. My heart was beating, pulsing like a panicked prey.

"My men will escort you outside Academy grounds."

Balefire stared at the Lion. "I will let you know when I've completed my investigations. *Any* breech of my grounds, by either you or your men, will be taken as a direct attack on my students, and myself, and I can assure you, I am not one of your Pride, nor am I a Lion, try your luck with me Kinraide, and I will take you to a place that's filled with many more of your kind....and I'll leave you there...burning in Hell."

With one savage glance at Kinraide's hand on Salome's arm, the Lion released his hold.

I stood frozen, staring at the man I'd thought was my enemy, but in this moment...was a friend.

"This way," the commander of Balefire's guards motioned.

Kinraide leaned close and glared at his niece. "You can't hide here forever, Salome. I'll be waiting. Pride law comes before anything else."

Then he was gone, striding through the door. Balefire went with them, leaving us behind. Salome trembled, before her knees unlocked. She fell, crumpling to the ground. I rushed forward, grasping her under her arms, as behind us came the rush of footsteps.

Nesrin pushed through the door, panicked eyes cutting straight to Salome. She wrapped her arms around the Lioness, replacing my hold. "I got you," she murmured. "Hold onto me, I got you."

I straightened and then turned. My hands were shaking by the time I reached for Ava and my Wolves. Tears blurred my vision, still I found them just the same, or they found me.

Either way I bowed my head and wept softly.

Heavy footsteps heading toward us made me stiffen.

Balefire stepped inside his office, scanning at everyone

there. Anger lingered in his movements as he rounded his desk, placed his hands in the middle and glared at Salome. "Now, Ms. Kinraide. I think you owe me a damn good explanation of what the Hell just happened...*and leave nothing out.*"

# CHAPTER TEN

## BIG BROTHER IS WATCHING

"WELL, YOU PRETTY MUCH KNOW IT ALL. KINRAIDE won't stop, not until he has me and the stone. He's always wanted to be King." Salome's voice hardened, and she curled her hands into fists in her lap. "So, I did what I had to do to survive." She tilted her head up, meeting Balefire's steely gaze. "That bastard killed my parents. He doesn't deserve to be anything."

"Everything," Balefire demanded.

Salome glanced to Ava, who gave a soft nod.

The Lioness turned back to the Principal, her words slow at first as she told him of the day Ava found her huddled against the Lodge, bleeding. She left nothing out, telling him about the hunter who came for her and then the spell that went wrong.

I sat there in silence, even when Ava muttered, "It's all true. I swear, you can't make this shit up." She stepped closer, desperation echoed in those blue eyes. I knew what was coming, knew that *manic* gleam in her eyes.

"Oh shit," I murmured as she started.

"I used my grandma's spell." Her words were a rush as

she stabbed a finger toward the Principal. "And, before you start on me, *yes,* I know magic is forbidden outside Witch clans, but we needed *something.* We were only trying to scare him, not... you know, turn him into a fish. You see grandma must have said *wish,* and I always thought it was *fish.* Thought it was weird, but never questioned it."

"Okay. *Okay*... I've heard enough," Balefire groaned and climbed to his feet. "You four..." He glared at Ava, Salome, Nesrin, and then me. "Come with me."

I wrenched a panicked look at Ava who paled, turning ashen, before I turned to Judas.

There was panic in his eyes as he searched mine. But that was his only reaction. He let me make the call...go with Balefire, or...not.

Balefire made for the door, turning the handle and striding through. Salome and Ava followed. My best friend's steps slowed...waiting for me.

Whatever we were in for...we'd handle it together.

I left the Wolves and Chuck behind and followed them out of the office and through the reception, before exiting into the hall.

There was no sign of Salome's uncle, only the sickening stench of mindless hunger he'd left behind.

"What do you think he did before he became a principal?" Ava whispered in my ear. "Maybe he was a mercenary, or even a stripper."

I cut her a sharp look. "Stripper?" I murmured under my breath.

Ava leaned closer to me. "Have you seen how buff those men get, and they work out insanely. Maybe he's taking steroids."

I laughed to myself and wrapped an arm around Ava,

drawing her against me, adoring how in any situation she made me laugh. "Never stop being yourself."

She blew me a kiss. "You got it, babe."

We halted outside a room, and Balefire dug his hand into his pocket before pulling out a set of jangling keys. He slid one into the lock, the clink loud.

"Um, what's behind the door?" Nesrin murmured, her hand in Salome's.

He pushed it open and walked in. We all stared inside at the four TV monitors lined up against the back wall, and each one was divided into quarters, showcasing a different part of the Academy grounds.

"Whoa, big brother is watching." Ava rushed inside first, and we followed. "Is this legal?"

"Did you read your contract when you first joined Bestias Academy?"

She huffed, facing the principal full of confidence. "Of course." She looked at me when he turned his attention back to the controls and shook her head.

I scanned the screens, and in the far left one was the lodge living room. Straining my eyes on the tiny image, I could swear my three Wolves stood there with Chuck, their backs facing away from me, but they were in a kind of huddled semi-circle, heads low staring at something.

"Give me a moment, ladies. I can't seem to find the right file."

I turned as he left the room, curious about what exactly he planned to show us, though knowing that it was somehow related to someone being taped had my stomach churning.

"O.M.G. they're comparing sizes," Ava spat.

I swung around to find her, Salome, and Nesrin gawking at the screen of the lodge.

"What?"

"I think I see some pink bits." Ava was pointing to the guys, still huddling and looking down at something, but the screen was too pixelated to make out exactly what they were doing.

"Eww." Nesrin scrunched her nose.

"They are not." I pushed myself past Salome and pressed my face practically to the screen. "You can't see anything."

"Then what are they doing?" Ava blurted.

"I don't know. They've caught something and they're all staring at it. Maybe they're checking out our new swords."

"Oh, they're checking out their swords all right." She burst out laughing.

"I think Ava's right on this one," Nesrin added. "Guys compare all the time. Maybe their sizes change weekly."

"Not sure that's right," Ava murmured. "They shrink in winter and expand in summer. Pretty sure that's how it works."

"Heard the one with the biggest dick ends up being the leader of gang, and this could be a reconfirmation that Judas remains alpha," Salome murmured, and everyone looked my way.

"What? You're all being ridiculous."

"I'm pretty sure Chuck would win, if that was the case," Ava teased and stuck her tongue at me.

"Eww eww, don't say crap like that around me. Told you before." My cheeks shouldn't have blushed, but they were on fire. I looked at the screen, and they were disbanding. "See they're heading off, it's nothing."

As they turned around to head for the doorway, Bond had his hand on his groin, adjusting himself.

"Ha," Ava yelled. "Did you see that. That proves it."

"Proves what?" Balefire's deep voice had us all jumping around, looking anywhere but the principal.

"Proves that you're doing an amazing job with all this secret spying," Ava replied and turned away from him.

"This isn't spying. The CCTV's monitor what happens on campus for security purposes and everyone's safety." He shut the door and only the screens lit up the room. Fiddling with the controls, the screen to the right flipped to white fuzzy lines before snapping back.

We watched the pond in the woods near school, and next to me, Ava fidgeted, shuffling on her feet and breathing fast.

A hand shot out of the slick water, and we all flinched. Ava released a tiny yelp. A man with yellow hair emerged from the pond, water dripping down his naked torso as he pushed out of the pond.

When he emerged to his hip, Ava made a cooing sound and Balefire moved lightning fast to place his hand over the man who stood there naked. He dropped to all fours, and suddenly golden fur sprouted over his body, his body growing, stretching, his jawline lengthening.

That looked painful, but no one said a word because with the three shifters in the room, this would seem natural to them. Balefire withdrew his hand when a lion now stood on the bank, his head tilted back as he released a silent roar... since there were no speakers. Then he strode out of the camera's line of sight.

"Shit!" Salome whispered.

Then the principle pressed buttons and the screen turned to static. Moments later, we were back to nearby woods, a distant image of Salome sitting on the ground, looking injured, while Ava ripped her pants for effect.

"God is that how I look in real life?" Ava cringed. "I need to lose twenty pounds, look at those chubby cheeks."

I smirked and turned to her, grabbing her cheeks between my fingers. "And they are adorable."

She batted me away, and we refocused on how she and Salome had wrestled with the hunter, then Ava was winding the man's hair around a twig, chanting something. He fell to the ground. One fin popped out of his side, followed by gills, and Nesrin made *ooh* sounds. In seconds, a golden fish flapped by their feet, and the girls dumped him in the pond.

Ava broke into a nervous laugh while Balefire glared her way.

"Why are you showing us this?" I asked.

"I've known about this for a while but was waiting for Ava and Salome to come forward with the truth following the recent events. When something like this happens, you need to come to me first, not try to solve everything on your own."

All of our faces paled, and my stomach might as well have dropped right through me and hit the ground at his confession. I exchanged nervous stares with Ava, and we knew... we both knew that eventually our secret would come out and we had to finally confess to our group of friends what we'd done. It should come from us.

"You can return to classes now," he instructed. "School goes on as normal for you, Salome, and I'll have extra guards around your dorm and classes."

"Thank you," was all she said. Nesrin looped her arm around her friend's and they both hightailed it out of the room, Ava on their heels.

Balefire turned back to the screen, switching the monitor we'd been watching back to monitoring mode.

I stayed behind, unable to move my feet. They locked in place. He glanced at me over his shoulder. "Is that all, Ms. Livingstone?"

"So, these CCTVs." I swallowed hard, my mind circling around the whole me killing Principal Stone, then Ava and I burying her in the woods thing. "Are they all over the Academy?"

He looked at me, trying to decipher the meaning behind my words, or maybe he already knew and waited for me to confess. But I couldn't. Wouldn't. I wanted to keep that secret buried, and I didn't want to stand trial in front of the council for defending myself.

"The grounds are under surveillance 24/7. I have eyes everywhere." Not another word from Balefire, but his gaze burrowed into me.

Sweat dripped down my spine at the heaviness between us, the silence. He knew. He freaking knew what Ava and I had done. I could see it in his eyes.

"Anything else," he asked.

"N...nope." I spun on my heels and hurried out there, finally breathing easy when I reached the foyer, finding Ava waiting for me. We ran out of the main building and darted to Chuck's, needing to finally come clean.

# CHAPTER ELEVEN

## THE WEIGHT OF IT ALL

I COULD HEAR THE PANIC INSIDE BEFORE I REACHED the door to Chuck's cottage. Anger lashed like a whip, covered by the muffled snarl that echoed from inside.

"You ready to do this?" Ava murmured beside me.

I stared at the door, and then exhaled long and hard. Secrets were stepping out of the shadows, and in Principal Stone's case they walked the damn hallways leaving grave dirt in their wake. "I guess I have a secret to share and it's better that it comes from me."

"And I thought I had it bad," Salome muttered behind me. "Seems we all have skeletons in our closet, don't we?"

We did, even if we never expected them to be there in the first place. I reached out, grasped the handle and turned the lock. Silence filled the room as I stepped inside. Ava, Nesrin, and Salome followed.

"What is it?" Judas turned toward me from pacing in the middle of the living room. "What's going on?"

The door closed behind us with a *thud*. Chuck moved forward, stopping in front of me and placing a massive hand on my arm. "Are you safe?"

I knew what he was asking. Was I in danger? Was I in need of protection? Did I need him to hurt, and maim...or kill? All I could do was nod. "No one is coming to hurt me. Not anymore."

"Then you want to fill us in on what the hell's going on?" Judas snarled.

"I do, but first...I just need to breathe, and look at you." I took a step closer and lifted my hand. Bond was the first to move and join us, stepping forward, capturing my grasp.

"You're scaring me," he whispered and searched my gaze.

"I'm okay." I smiled and clenched his hand. "Okay, this is going to be a shock. So Principal Stone was murdered and buried here in the school grounds." I glanced over my shoulder to Ava before I turned back to them. "And I'm the one who killed her."

"What the Hell?" Judas murmured.

But Bond never wavered, instead he searched my gaze.

"It was an accident," I answered. "I swear to you. She attacked me out of nowhere. I wasn't prepared..."

"Who is," Bond muttered, staring at the ground.

"Ava and I buried her in the cemetery. We did our best to cover it up."

"Wait a minute," Judas said. "Was this before, or after the dance?"

"Before." I held his gaze. "I never meant for it to happen."

"I'm sorry I wasn't there for you, Morwenna." Chuck shook his head. Anger filled his eyes. "I failed you."

"You didn't fail anyone." Ava left my side, stepping close to wrap her arms around him.

All heads turned, and mouths opened—I realized it was

the first time anyone had an inkling of what was happening between them.

"You were sick. The *whole* Vampire race was sick. Besides, Mor is stronger than you think."

There was a shake of Judas' head. "She shouldn't have to be." When he lifted his head and looked at me, I saw the truth of *what he saw*. I was someone he felt responsible for, someone he needed to protect, to hold tight...as tight as he could.

"I'm okay." I lifted my hands and met his gaze, and then slowly moved to Chuck. "I'm more than okay. I had Ava. But I'm not telling you this so you can get angry with yourselves, or me. I'm telling you this because Balefire knows. He took us to a room filled with security equipment. He showed us the footage of when Ava and Salome put that shifter into the pond as a fish."

Heads turned as they glanced to Salome, and then Ava, still I continued. "He made it perfectly clear the entire school was under surveillance, and without coming outright and saying it, he let me know he'd seen the footage of me and Principal Stone."

The temperature in the room dropped in an instant. Cold, steely gazes from the Wolves and Chuck. I knew what they were thinking. Their first instinct was to protect. Panic raced through me. While they plotted to protect me, I was scrambling to think of ways to protect them. "He's had it for a while, and I don't think he has plans to investigate it further."

"How can you be sure?" Chuck growled and dropped his hand from around Ava.

Love and honor collided in his gaze. His hand fisted at his side. One word was all it'd take. One simple word and I'd unleash a Vampire deadlier that I'd ever be. "I can't be sure, but, I know men like Balefire." I stepped toward Chuck, reaching out to touch that clenched fist at his side. "I was raised by men like Balefire. Shrewd men, careful men. I know how they think. If Balefire was going to do anything to harm me, then why show me his hand? Why bring me in there and let me see what he has?"

The warrior stilled, dark eyes searching mine. "What if he has no honor? What if this was all a setup, something designed to shake you."

"Then I become unshakeable." I held strong. "But this isn't about me. This is about Salome...Balefire has the footage. He knows what happened."

"Still, he can't do a damn thing," Salome answered for me. "My uncle won't give up, not until he takes what he wants, by force if he has to."

"Then we take him out?" Bond answered. "We go in there, kill the sonovabitch, and be done with it."

"It's not that easy," the defeated words slipped from her lips.

"*It is that easy,*" Bond snarled. He was unflinching, blue eyes boring into the wall of the living room. I'd never seen him this angry, this...*consumed.* "No girl should be controlled like that. No girl deserves to be used like she's nothing."

He turned then, wrenching his gaze away.

"Bond." I reached for him as he cut across the living room and headed for the kitchen.

But there was no stopping him, no reaching him. In that moment he was lost. I glanced to Judas who just shook his head, glanced at Nero, and jerked his head toward the kitchen.

Nero followed, disappearing through the doorway as Nesrin answered behind me. "So, we stay together, for as long as we can. We protect Salome, until the end. I'm not letting you go without a fight." She lifted her hand, and Salome met the Panther's grip with her own, turning toward her. "I won't let them take you. Not now, not after we've found each other."

I swallowed hard as Nesrin pulled Salome closer, wrapping her arms around her tight. Soft, muffled cries echoed as they held onto each other. My throat thickened, shoulders curled. I felt heavy, weighed down by it all.

Judas turned and grasped the folders taken from the hidden room under the church floor. Dust fell from the edges. I strode forward and brushed my hand along his arm as he met my gaze.

"There has to be something we can do," he whispered and glanced to Nesrin and Salome. "There *has to be.*"

I wanted there to be, more than I wanted anything else. The folder blurred in his hand. I stared at the filthy pages as a tear slipped from my eye and raced down my cheek.

As the sound of sobbing echoed through the room, I closed my eyes...and prayed for a miracle.

# CHAPTER TWELVE

## FUCK PRIDE LAW

The hallway was full of students. Bodies pushing past me as I made my way toward class.

But I didn't see them, not really.

I was stuck inside my thoughts. Trapped by the constant replay of Nesrin and Salome's gut-wrenching sobs. Ava followed close behind, shoving forward, head down, not saying much at all.

The files filled my mind. I tried to look at them, tried to find something we could use. But in the end, I gave up. They were just words on a page, nothing more, nothing less.

No hope.

No salvation.

No... nothing.

"Hey." Ava grabbed my wrist, yanking me out of the rush of students. "You passed our class." She glanced over at the door several feet away.

"I think the entire Academy is in this hallway," I muttered as Judas and Bond stepped out from the crowd.

Nero stood farther down the hall, turning on the spot, lost, and Ava just shook her head.

"Class?" Ava urged and glanced at the open door.

"Actually, I think I have a class with Leathers," I murmured. "I'll catch you guys a little later."

Ava's brow narrowed. "You don't have an Understudy class."

"I do now." I forced a smile. "Just meet me later, okay?"

I turned away from her, leaving my best friend and my Wolves staring after me as I stepped back into the rush of students hurrying to class.

Nerves settled deep. I'd not seen Nefarious since the meeting with the mortals, even then he'd been quiet, withdrawn from me...like he was scared of me. I slowed at his door, lifted my hand, and knocked gently.

Movement came from inside. There was the scrape of a chair, soft footsteps followed. I waited as Mr. Leathers opened the door and met my gaze. Surprise widened his eyes. "Morwenna... I was wondering when I was going to see you."

"Mr. Leathers. I hope this is okay."

"Of course." He stepped to the side, glancing at the other students in the hallway as I passed him, and then he closed the door behind us.

The classroom was as quiet as always, but open on Nefarious' desk was a laptop. I stepped through the rows of unused seats and stopped, catching him paused in the middle of what looked like a news broadcast. "I hope I'm not disturbing you."

"No." He hurried forward and closed the screen. "Not at all. What can I do for you?"

"I just wanted to make sure you were okay. I've not had any Understudy lessons scheduled."

There was a wince, before he cleared his throat. "Yes, well...about that."

"You're afraid of me, aren't you?"

He stiffened, eyes riveted on the desk and not on me. "You've exceeded our expectations."

"With the Witch storm?"

There was a nod. "Yes, that and other. The Ancient...he's unsure what to do with you."

"Unsure what to do with me?" Anger rose to the surface. "I'm trying to keep my family together...and my friends. I'm trying to do what the Ancient asked of me...what else can I do?"

There was a hard sigh before Nefarious met my gaze. "Family is one thing, but an entire clan needs you, Morwenna. In the role of Understudy, you must look past the events in front of you to see the bigger picture. I want to show you something."

He rounded the end of his desk and opened the laptop he'd closed before, the same news report still paused in the middle. He reached out, tapped the spacebar and the news woman kept talking.

*"This is the second murder in as many months. Police are baffled, but with ties to the seedy underbelly of the Tricks City Vampire community, they're looking into this as a serial murderer. A Vampire serial murderer."*

I flinched at the words. "Another murder?"

"Yes." He closed the laptop once more. "And this time with a warning."

He pulled out a photo from under a stack of books. A mortal man was dead, head turned, glazed eyes staring into the camera. But it was his neck I stared at. The flesh torn open, veins shredded.

Another photo followed, and even though my stomach clenched at the sight, I made myself look. It was a close up of the wound, fang marks evident. Another followed, this time of the words written in blood.

"Give her back to me?" I glanced at the writing and lifted my head. "This...doesn't look like a serial killer to me."

Nefarious took the photo from my grasp. "No, it doesn't. But it could be."

"And no one has any idea who this is?"

"Not yet. There's talk of immortal underground fighting rings, places where even people working for your father are afraid to go. Greed, power, those are the commodities they trade in. They demand blood in return. These are dangerous people, Morwenna, and their reach knows no bounds. Some believe the person responsible belongs to these groups."

"But it could also just be someone just killing for blood too?"

He nodded.

"And you expect me to, what, find the one responsible and shut it down?" I gasped.

He just shook his head. "We did, before we understood what we were dealing with. Now we need you to be the Vampire we need. To keep the mortals from waging a war on our community, until the heads of the clans get together to stop this once and for all."

"But it's only a couple of murders," I explained. "People kill just as many of each other, more even."

He sighed. "Yes, but when a Vampire kills a human, the media exaggerates the stories and people panic. A few blood supplies stop, and then Vampires will panic. We want to put an end to it before the fear takes hold."

It was all too much. Too overwhelming. Too over my head. I stared at my hands. "How can I help an entire community, when I can't even help one person?"

"What are you talking about?"

I tried to gather myself, tried to find the strength to keep from going under. "I came here for advice for a friend. A Lioness."

"Salome Kinraide," he answered with a nod. "I heard what's going on, and I'm sorry."

"I don't want your sympathy. I want your advice. I want your guidance. I want you to tell me there's a way out of this for her."

"Pride law isn't like Vampire law. They don't have the numbers we have, or the opportunities. They kill, they claim, they take. I've studied all immortal laws, and I'm sorry to tell you, that unless there's another male in a powerful pride she can marry instead, there's not much hope for her."

My stomach tightened, heart grew heavy. "She can run."

"And stay running the rest of her life."

"At least she'll have a life." I lifted my head, meeting his gaze.

There was sadness in his eyes. "Pride law—"

I rose from the corner of the desk. "Fuck Pride law. Fuck any law that says who a woman must marry, or who she can't. *She* should be enough just as she is. *She* shouldn't give a damn if she doesn't meet expectations. *She* is a force to be reckoned with."

He was silent now.

Just as they should all be silent.

I strode from between the empty desks and made my way to the door. The hallways were empty. Hellhound guards stood sentry outside closed classroom doors.

The first one shifted as I neared.

The second curled his lips in a snarl.

The third opened his mouth to bark orders.

I just lifted my hand and channeled my inner Ava, flipping him the bird as I strode past. I headed along the empty hallway and shoved through the front doors. Heavy footsteps leading me on. Dark, bruised clouds gathered overhead, thunder rumbled a warning in the distance.

I felt like the sky... battered and hurt for Salome.

I could imagine how terrible the Lioness must feel, trapped. I wanted to scream at the unfairness, but I'd find no answer in that.

I found myself heading toward the Lodge, past the spot where Ava found Salome, and climbed the front steps. Cool air flowed around me as I pushed open the front door and stepped inside. I couldn't sit in a damn classroom. Couldn't force myself to concentrate. Not when my mind hurt, and my stomach churned. I needed to find an answer, needed something other than sitting back and feeling sorry for Salome, for myself. I palmed open the door to a welcoming waft of coffee, dragged myself over to the vending machines in the hallway and aimed for the blood latte button but changed at the last minute and jabbed the blood cappuccino. Today called for extra milky froth.

Sipping the warm drink in my hands, I strolled along the back room, studying the shelves of books covering mostly historical facts about the Academy, packs, clans and other mundane facts on the supernatural. A place I'd normally find dull, but recently this location had been my go to for information. Dust coated the books and the bright light overhead threw an orange tinge over everything in the room.

Finally hitting upon Pride law, I pulled two volumes out and carried them to the main room, balancing my cup in the other hand.

I dropped the books on the small table with a thump and reclined on the couch, throwing back the rest of the blood cappuccino before wiping away the foamy mustache.

The lodge remained empty, and I enjoyed the peace. Since beginning Bestias Academy, I'd been in a whirlwind of activity and dangers. So, there was something calming, soothing, about being alone for a change.

I flipped open one of the books, *Pride Matters*. Page after page of tiny print spelling out which Alpha led which Pride, what date and country. I kept flipping until I reached the back and found no appendix. *Great.*

In the next volume, the topic changed to how to treat enemies that invade territory, and while interested, it wasn't what I was searching for. So, I carried those back and scanned the spines of yet more books. *Warfare. Catching Prey. Taking Territory. Mating.* When I reached the bottom row, I knelt and read the titles sideways.

*Achoo. Achoo. Achoo.*

Damn dust was tickling my nose. Then I saw the words, *Pride Families*, and curiosity had me pulling the book out.

Lugging it over to the main room, I blew the layered dust off the leather cover and searched for Kinraide, curious what I could find on Salome's family. Anything to give me more information.

Leon Kinraide. Longest serving noble Pride family in history, known for his military precision attacks.

The paragraph waffled on and on about his achievements along with having forty-three sons. Okay, maybe he was Salome's grandfather or an older ancestor, but her family was well respected and a freaking noble one.

But the more I read, the heavier my eyes grew. I flipped over the next few pages when my gaze caught on a familiar name.

*Arson Arlo.*

I rolled the name over in my mind, and it hit me like a brick. His name was in the underground Academy files. He was a lion shifter too? Interesting, but like Leon, the book only talked about the Alpha's achievements. Slapping the book shut, I heaved a heavy sigh and figured this was a dead end.

# CHAPTER THIRTEEN

## DOWN TO THE MATTS

I PUSHED OUT OF THE DOORWAY, LEAVING THE LODGE behind. My mind was filled with names...useless names. There had to be a way out of this. Something I wasn't seeing.

Something right in front of me.

As I walked back to the main building, a flash of white followed, before the Demon bunny let out a hideous screech and scurried further into the trees. The breeze picked up, casting the deep, savage scent of male and Lion. I wrinkled my nose and stopped in the middle of the path. The scent grew stronger. The longer I stood here, the more vulnerable I felt. Hairs stood on my arms as movement came from the trees. I could smell them out there, waiting... hunting. I took a step, but it wasn't toward the main building, or behind me to the Lodge. It was to the trees, facing the scum who wanted control.

"I'm not scared of you, not any of you. I'll find a way out of this for Salome. I swear to you...you'll never control her. You'll never touch her. Not if I can help it."

There was no movement in the trees, but a low grow rumbled on the wind.

I forced myself not to run, but to walk slowly all the way back to the main building.

The bell rang for the next class as the door closed behind me. I stumbled to the wall and leaned into the corner, taking long, hard breaths. My hands were trembling, still I clenched my fist, willing the shaking away, and then headed to the gymnasium.

I hurried into the women's changing room, and quickly opened my locker. One careful glance over my shoulder and I took off my shirt and skirt, changing into roomy sweat shorts and a soft, hugging t-shirt. I stashed them away before I hurried from the change room and into the hall.

Combat class had already started. The other students were gathered on the floor mats around our instructor. I rushed inside and glanced back at the door swinging shut. My nerves were shot to hell, the hairs on my arms still standing on end. Ava turned her head toward me, and then shifted over, making room as I hurried over.

Salome and Nesrin sat toward the back of the class, staring at anything but Mr. Marlow who stood in the middle of the circle.

"Now, not all shifters are graced with agility. The trick is to not just find your strengths, but also *your opponent's weaknesses*. Hunting, combat, they're just the same. They're your prey, and you're searching for a way to take them down."

Mr. Marlow raised his gaze to look at me as I crumpled next to Ava.

"Nice of you to join us, Ms Livingstone."

"Sorry, Sir. I was coming back from the Lodge."

One nod of his head and all was forgiven.

"So," he continued. "I want you to remember, it's more about your opponent than it ever is about you."

There was a snarl, then a scuffle from the Wolves. I didn't need to lift my head to see who it was.

"Take Mr. Blackthorne here." Mr. Marlow straightened.

Thick muscles bulged under our instructor's too-tight camouflage t-shirt and stretched tight sweatpants. Ava just stared.

"Ava, you're drooling," I murmured.

"Sure, he's fast and strong. But he's cocky."

Judas forced a smile as Nero gave him a jab. But Bond wasn't smiling. He was staring straight ahead with the same steely gaze he'd had last night. I didn't look at Judas, even when I felt the weight of his gaze, desperate to draw mine.

"So, let's see if there's someone who can take all that I've taught you this past semester and beat him."

There was a snigger, and a soft cheer echoed through the rest of the class as Mr. Marlow motioned his hand toward the Alpha.

He glanced my way before he took a step, striding through the gap in the circle and taking his place, center stage.

I gave Bond one last glance, and then turned to Judas. He watched me, like he was proud or something.

"Any takers?" Mr. Marlow growled.

"I'll go." One of the Ghoul's raised his hand and pushed to stand.

*Ooo's* rippled through the air as Furley Stone stepped between Nesrin and Salome and stopped in the middle of the mat.

"Well, alright," our instructor murmured. "Strength versus agility."

Judas curled his top lip as Furley smiled and glanced

around the class. Mr. Marlow took a step backwards, easing off the mat. We all stood, knowing exactly what was going to happen, and there was no way I was getting trampled; especially not by a Ghoul.

The attack started without me watching. Furley gave a savage snarl and lunged, driving every pound of his massive weight forward.

But Judas was ready. Strength and weight had nothing on the cunning Alpha. He lunged, narrowly missing the swipe of a massive hand as Furley charged.

The floor thundered, Ava winced as Judas rounded the Ghoul's back and wrenched his foot into the air, driving it against his backside.

Momentum took the poor guy. But Furley wasn't done yet, catching his stumble on the edge of the mat before he turned. "Is that all you got, Blackthorne?"

There was a snigger from someone, and that was all Judas needed. He lifted his arms and shrugged.

With a guttural roar, Furley charged again, this time taking it slower, and watching Judas's every movement. He swung, taking Judas by surprise, landing a blow on the side of his head. The Wolf dropped to one knee, and then sprang back up as the Ghoul's arm sailed overhead for a second hit but missed.

The big guy wasn't as dumb as everyone thought, earning a cheer from his friends on the side-lines. Then he made the biggest mistake, he turned to the Wolf—and became cocky.

There was a smile and a snigger as he glanced at the Kitsune shifter he was dating. She squealed, the smile dying on her face as Judas reared behind him and grasped his outstretched arm.

The move was fast. Judas moved well...for a Wolf—but

he was soft and fluid. Not driven by a seething river of untapped rage, unlike how I'd seen Chuck fighting on a few occasions.

As I watched Judas yank the Ghoul forward, pulling his center of gravity out from under him, I knew just how dangerous Judas truly was. I turned toward Ava as the heavy *thud* followed...and the quake tore along the floor.

Ava winced, watching Judas.

"Well done, Mr. Blackthorne, seems agility has won again, in this instance," Mr. Morley muttered and stepped up onto the mat.

Furley moaned as he slowly pushed to stand. I caught the movement from the corner of my eye as yet another male stepped forward onto the mats to challenge Judas. I watched him this time, not just his movements or the way his eyes tracked movement like a moth tracks the light. But in the way he was all coiled muscle, all hunger and need.

There was a lunge, and a swipe. This opponent was a new guy, a Wolf, just like Judas. But there was a difference in the way they stood.

The new guy was bigger than Judas, just like the Ghoul, almost as muscled as Bond, but not quite. He sprung into the air from a standstill to collide with Judas.

They were on the ground, all arms and muscled thighs rippling with the need to pin the other to the ground. There was a grunt, a roll, and in an instant the new guy was on the bottom.

"That's hot." One of the other girls in the class watched with interest, dark eyes sparkling with desire.

Jealously plunged me into an icy abyss. I clenched my jaw, watching the way she grazed her teeth along her bottom lip and stared at them.

*"Tap out,"* Judas growled at the Beta.

*Thump...thump...*and with a low, painful whine, followed by a bark of resignation. "Let me up... *I said, let me the Hell up.*"

Judas lifted his arms, rolled, and backed away.

"Seems like we have ourselves an undefeated champion," Mr. Morley muttered and crossed his arms.

But this was all a male show of pride, just a game... wasn't it always? *Push you down, make you marry...make you yield.* "I'll challenge." I turned to Mr. Morley and took a step toward the mat.

"What?" Judas smiled and shook his head.

But I kept walking, stepping up onto the cushioned blue floor.

"Ms. Livingstone," our instructor started, casting a panicked glance to Judas. "I don't think this is appropriate."

"Why?" I tried to capture his gaze, but he was looking at everyone else but me.

No one saw me...*no one saw us.*

"Fuck, yeah," Nesrin growled. "Now we have a real fight."

Judas let out a bark and stepped closer, meeting me on the edge of the mat. "Mor." He reached for my hand, fingers brushing against my skin. "I don't think this is the place."

"You afraid of a Vampire, *Wolf?*" I gave him my sweetest smile. "I promise...I'll take it easy on you...*at first.*"

Panic flared for a second in those brown eyes, until there was a curl of the corner of his lips. "Really think you're that good, huh?"

It was my turn to shrug. "I dunno, wanna find out?"

I knew damn well I was. Vampire...and whatever remnant power the Queen of Witches, Hekate had left behind raged through every cell of my body. I wasn't just one or the other. I was both, and it was about damn time he saw me for the hunter I was.

"I'm not happy about this," Mr. Morley snapped.

"I'm not asking you to be," I said, never once taking my eyes off the Wolf in front of me.

With a loud, exhausted sigh the teacher gave up.

"Judas," Bond warned.

"It's okay." The Alpha held up his hand. "I got this. I won't hurt her."

"Won't hurt me?" I murmured and stepped away as he tried to flank my side. "I always knew you were a little forgetful, but maybe you need a gentle reminder of who you're actually dealing with."

I lunged then, driving every ounce of power I had into my thighs and cleared half of the mat in an instant. Judas lifted his head, but he just stood there, like the biggest goof-ball, kind of stunned as I landed hard, driving him to the ground.

He grabbed me, pulling me close in a vice like hug, and wrapped his legs around mine before we rolled, pinning me to the ground. "Hell, you're sexy when you're like this." He stared into my eyes.

"Really?" I murmured and drove my feet to the floor as I thrust my hips and pivoted.

He shot straight upwards, losing his grip for a second. A second was all I needed. I wound my arm under his and clenched tight, pushing forward to slam him onto his back with an *oof*.

One shift of my arms and I gripped his wrists, slamming them to the ground above his head. The boom of his heart filled my ears. His body twitched underneath me, hardening in places it shouldn't...not for an opponent anyway.

*Only for me.*

"Do you yield?" I growled.

Those brown eyes gripped me. He was all in for surrender. One thrust of my hips and I hooked my feet against the insides of his, forcing his legs to widen, and his growing thickness to press harder between my legs. "Do...you...yield?"

"I yield," he whispered, but I doubt he had any idea he spoke. "Just don't...move straight away."

Mr. Morley cleared his throat. "W-well," he stuttered. "This has been interesting. Seems our Mr. Blackthorne isn't the only Alpha in the classroom."

All Judas could do was shake his head, but I caught the smile tugging on his lips. "First you bring ghosts back to life, then you hand me my ass in the one damn thing I was good at. What's next, Mor?"

I froze at his words. "What did you just say?"

"What?" he murmured. "About you handing me my ass? You want me to say it again? Fine, you beat me, fair and square—"

"No." I eased my grip from his wrists and sat up. "About bringing ghosts back to life."

He pushed up on his elbows, not caring that the entire class was still staring at us. "You bought your roommate back to life, didn't you? And that asshole, Brutus."

"That's it." I shoved upwards. He winced when I just miss his erection with my knee, but I couldn't think about his desire now...all I could think about was one massive piece of the puzzle slipping into place.

I stood tall before I turned to Salome. "I know how to stop you from having to marry your uncle."

# CHAPTER FOURTEEN

## RAINBOW PLUS

"Mor, slow down," Bond called out.

"Hurry up, slow poke," Ava teased as we all raced away from the gym and across the lawn. Students gawked at the seven of us making haste.

Behind us, Bond was dragging his black collared tee over his head, before pulling it down over his firm chest, his ripped abs, and I drooled a bit. But I shoved those thoughts aside. I had a lead... A possible solution to help Salome. And I'd do anything to help her, so that took priority.

I gripped Salome's wrist, drawing her with me.

"Back to your guard's place?" Nesrin muttered. "Really?"

"We need somewhere that we can all get together." Ava cut her a glare. "Balefire's guards are everywhere we damn well turn."

"Sure," Nero murmured. "It has nothing to do with the dangerous as fuck Vampire living there."

Ava huffed. "Don't know what you're talking about. My Chuck wouldn't hurt a fly. Trust me."

The small house sat apart from the towering dormitories. Smoke curled from the chimney, the smell of burning wood on the air. Excitement buzzed inside my head. I was desperate to spill what I thought might work.

I hurried to the front door, twisted the handle and pushed inside. "Chuck...Chuck, I have an idea."

The sickly, hot metallic scent of blood filled the air.

Stealing my thoughts...

*Stealing everything.*

I inhaled hard, drawn to the scent by that primal need inside, the need for food...the need to survive. Pain stabbed my gums. My fangs grew, tongue flicked out, skirting my lips. *"Chuck?"*

He was on his hands and knees in the middle of the kitchen. Crimson coated his hands, frothing with a mass of soap and water as he scrubbed the floorboards.

He jerked his head up, dark eyes glinting as I rounded the entrance and stopped cold.

The smell was inescapable, crawling in my nose, making me swallow and swallow...*and swallow.*

The cold, emotionless stare I'd seen so many times gripped mine as he wrung the cloth into the bucket in front of him, and then slowly.... *meticulously,* dried his hands. "I wasn't expecting company."

"We can see that," Nesrin murmured.

No one said a word. Not a question, not a whimper.

I glanced to Ava who stared at the mess on the floor. There was a rule in our house, one I'd grown up with my entire life...*don't ask questions, especially if you're not prepared for the truth.* The look in her eyes said she wasn't ready to hear what he had to say.

I swallowed hard and took a step as he grabbed the bucket of bloody, soapy water and dumped the contents down the sink.

"So, are we doing this?" I whispered, and then turned to others. "Do you want to hear a way out of this for Salome?"

They all nodded, even as they stared at Chuck, who wrung blood from his cloth. Then they slowly turned and wandered into the living room.

Bond dragged over the single seater chair, lugging a small rug with it, and squished the couch between Bond and Nesrin's seats at the table before flopping down.

Ava looked around the room and cocked her head to the side. "Where's Jubba?"

"Locked in the bedroom," Chuck muttered, wringing things in the kitchen. "Where the vermin need to be. He chewed through my toothpaste, did I tell you that? I can still smell mint scented poop."

"Can you let him out, pretty please."

Several moments later, Jubba was rushing into the room, his gaze taking in everyone.

"So," I began, unable to stop focusing on the noise of wringing water from the kitchen. "Thought we could talk about—"

"We need a group name," Ava announced, settling in her seat with Jubba in her lap, patting him. "If this is going to be our meeting point from now on, then we should have a name."

"I don't think that's necessary," I answered.

"Eight pillars," she murmured, ignoring me.

"Favoreight," Nero added.

"Sounds like a soft drink," Nesrin murmured. "I prefer Eight Bad Ass."

"Do we really need a name?" I asked, and everyone shot a look my way as if *this* was important. "Let's focus on the main reason we're here."

"Excellent." Ava flexed her fingers.

Judas coughed, "GR8."

"I'll make coffee." Chuck called out.

I cleared my throat. "Okay, so I think I found a way to help Salome. Thanks to Judas."

"Was that before, or after you wiped the floor with him?" Nero chuckled, earning a snarl from Judas.

"According to Pride law, if Salome married another male in a more powerful Pride, she'd be safe from marrying her uncle."

"You want me to marry a stranger?" Her posture stiffened, and she glanced over to Nesrin.

The room was quiet. I felt the weight of their gazes...and the tide when it started to turn.

"That won't work." Salome shook her head.

I took a step toward her. "Hear me out."

Chuck entered the room, carrying a tray of cups of coffee. "Wasn't sure what anyone wanted, so I added a bit of cream and sugar for everyone." He set one in front of me. "Blood in yours."

I grabbed the cup. "Thanks."

"So, who do you have in mind?" Nesrin asked.

"Arson Arlo."

"What?" Salome blurted. "You mean *dead* Arson Arlo?"

"The file from the hidden cave?" Ava, still holding Jubba, sidled up next to Chuck. Her arms brushed his, earning a brooding stare.

"I went to see Mr. Leathers and talked to him about a few things." I glanced toward the kitchen, and where the pool of blood used to be as the news report came to life inside my head. "He told me about Pride law, so I went to the Lodge to investigate."

"On your own, Mor?" Judas growled. "We've been through this. We stick together, right?"

I gave him a smile. "I know... I was just frustrated. When I searched Pride families I found the Arlo pride. They're respected, almost feared."

"Were," Salome murmured. "Until their line was cut short."

"Exactly." I held her gaze. "Which is why Arson is perfect."

"Except, he's dead," Nesrin repeated.

"Yes, *but* the Witch storm brought Brutus and Cassidy closer to life. What if I could bring Arson back too?" I sat on the edge of my seat.

"You're talking about some kind of necromancy." Nero shook his head. "That's not something you want to play with, Mor."

"I've already played with it, if you've forgotten." I held his stare. No one knew what it felt like to walk on the other side of darkness more than I did. No one felt that chill you just couldn't shake, or that brush of death...*whispering your name*. Even with Hekate's hold on me gone, I still felt power brewing inside me, just underneath the the skin.

I lifted my hand, fingers brushing the hollow in my chest. A different kind of power lay inside me, but was it me...or was it Hekate?

Nesrin cleared her throat. "It's better than nothing."

Salome nodded. "I'll try anything." The rest of the gang nodded.

And for once, everyone agreed.

"Where do we start?" Judas asked, lowering his hand to my thigh.

Brown eyes met mine, and I clung to the spark of life, as hard as I could. "We start with him... *Arson.*"

"I'll grab the files," Salome murmured, and suddenly

every eye was on me. "We find your new roommate and we find Arson."

I finished my coffee and climbed to my feet. "She might know if Arson is walking around and how to connect with him."

Salome, Ava, and Nesrin were up, ready to join me. Ava brushed Chuck's hand and gave him a smile. "Let's do this."

"With Balefire's guards around the grounds, it's best if just us four girls go find Cassidy in the dorms," I suggested, and Judas nodded.

We left Chuck and the Wolves in a flurry, no words exchanged, just rapid movement. When we reach the ground floor of our dorm building, a tall figure stepped out from the shadows.

"Why aren't you in class?" the Hellhound guard snarled, hands gripping his hips, his restless gaze swinging across the four of us. "There's no one permitted in the dorms during class."

"Since when?" Ava blurted.

"I'm not feeling well." I reached for my stomach.

But he was already rolling his eyes. "Get back to class."

I stiffened, my mouth falling open with a response, but it was Nesrin who moved forward, strong, her chin tilted up.

Her skin started to shimmer, and a deep guttural growl rolled in her chest. Nesrin's eyes glinted like golden cat eyes, her lips curling over extended fangs.

Ava joined Nesrin, her body shaking, and hell, she was going to release her Kraken!

"You don't want to get in our way," I warned.

The Hellhound's bushy brows knotted together, and hesitation washed over his face.

"Get the hell out of the way," Nesrin snarled.

No one moved, but when Salome and I lined up with Ava and Nesrin to face the guard, he released an exhale, his shoulders dropping.

"Fine, go, but don't be long. You don't want Principal Balefire to see you're missing."

We didn't wait a second longer, rushing upstairs and into my room.

"Cassidy," I called out, with the three girls doing the same. Ava searched for her in the bathroom. I spun on the spot, waiting for her to pop out of the walls or somewhere.

Ava flopped onto the bed. "She's not here. Do you have any chocolate?"

"No, you'll have to hit the vending machine." I turned around, searching for any sign of the ghost. "Cassidy, I've got some amazing Madonna music we can listen to?"

Fifteen minutes of waiting and she'd made no show. Ava was already pulling open the door. "If we're waiting around for her, we need chocolate."

Salome and Nesrin headed out as well, so I followed.

"Cassidy," I whispered in the hallway as we headed in the opposite direction from where the guard had been hiding. Downstairs, Ava was jabbing at the vending machine, and I rubbed my chin while studying the hot blood machine; my choices were coffee or hot chocolate.

I reached for the button when a scratchy noise came from the machine like a mouse scurried inside.

"Did you hear that?" Salome was leaning behind the machine, searching when the sound came again, louder and this time clearly from behind the nearby basement door.

We all exchanged glances, and I moved closer to the door.

"I'm not going in there," Ava murmured. "I vote Nesrin investigates."

She scrunched her nose. "No, thank you."

"It's probably another ghost." Salome didn't move away from the vending machine.

Ava collected her chocolate then joined me. "What do you think?" I said.

"On three?" She stuffed the chocolate into her pocket.

I took a deep breath and both of us reached for the handle. Before she even started counting, we both yanked opened the door, my skin rippling with dread.

We backed away, expecting something... anything. But instead we found only a dim room, and sitting inside on a wooden crate was Cassidy, dragging her shackle across the concrete floor. I'd recognize that nest-like hairstyle anywhere.

I stepped inside, and she lifted her gaze and stared at me. "I was wondering when you were finally going to put it all together."

# CHAPTER FIFTEEN

### EMOTIONAL VAMPIRES SUCK!

"Did you know about the situation with Salome?" I stepped closer.

"Suspected more like it. Especially after I heard you talking to the tone deaf one." She glanced at Ava.

"I am not tone deaf."

"Sure sounds like it when you sing." The ghost shrugged.

There was a snarl behind me, savage and fierce. I stepped to the side, putting myself in the firing line between the pissed off Kraken and the ghost with an attitude.

"If you knew then, why didn't you come to me?" I asked

"You didn't need me, or my help."

"Is that what this is about?" I slowly knelt, staring at the mass of knots in her matted hair. "Is this payback? Sorry. There's so much going on that I was rude before, and I shouldn't have brushed you off."

She just gave a shrug. "I wanted to be friends with you. I've never had a roommate before, not one like you."

"I'd love to be friends too, and we can be," I murmured. "We know you're Arson's friend too."

She sighed at the name and shot her gaze to mine, and for a second, she wavered, fading a little, like a washed-out version of the weird roommate I knew. "So how did you find out about Arson..."

Salome was the one who stepped forward. "He was the son of a King."

Sadness filled Cassidy's gaze and she twitched with the words. I could see she was fighting the memories.

"You were friends, right? I read that in a file. Were you dating...is that why?"

A hard snort tore from Cassidy's nose. "Dating? You read that in the file, huh?" She shook her head. "Well, sorry to tell you this, but your file is wrong. Arson and I weren't dating. We were just friends."

Something wasn't adding up, something she was hiding. "But you were killed together, right? That's what you told me. Down there in the basement." I glanced past her to the darkness.

"Yes," her voice softened, she swallowed hard, shifting where she sat. "We were."

"By Brutus," I pushed her, and I hated pushing her, but I had to understand.

She met my gaze, anger and pain flaring in those washed out green eyes. "Yes, because I didn't love him."

"What?"

She met my gaze, anger and hate curling her lips. The color in her cheeks became brighter, the outline of her body more solid than I'd ever seen her before. "He hated me because I wouldn't love him...and I wouldn't love him...because I didn't like guys, not in that way."

There was a whimper behind me. I didn't need to turn my head to know it was Nesrin.

"Goddamn bastard," the Panther snarled.

"He used to hurt me, pull my hair, tease me. One day he...he...he cornered me in a classroom and tried to push his hand up my skirt."

The savage snarl behind me stopped cold.

"Arson was like me. He didn't like women, not in a romantic sense. So, we gravitated to each other, went to our school dance together. We even held hands when Brutus was watching...but it wasn't romantic like that. We were just friends."

"And that's why he died? Because he was protecting you?"

She gave a slow nod. "There was a note on my bed from Lucy Orion. She was a Vampire, a beautiful, funny, quirky girl I liked. I used to sit behind her in class just, so I could smell the hairspray she used... The note asked me if I'd meet her here." She looked over her shoulder and then dropped her gaze. "Down there, actually. I went, not thinking. So stupid. But she wasn't there. Brutus was. He hit me on the back of the head, knocked me out cold, and when I came to, I had these."

She lifted her hand, the shackles sliding down her wrist. "I couldn't move, couldn't cry for help...I couldn't do anything. But somehow Arson found me. He came tearing down the stairs and tried to get me free. But I couldn't scream. Brutus was bleeding me dry."

I glanced to her neck. There were no fang marks.

"Of emotion." She stared into my eyes. "Every bit of me felt like I was dying. Anger, sadness...love, grief it was all just slipping away. I felt nothing."

"An Emotional Vampire?" I whispered. "Is that what he's called?"

She just nodded. "The worst kind of Vampire."

And for once I agreed with her.

"And this *Brutus* killed Arson for being your friend?" Salome murmured.

Cassidy just nodded. "He said if he couldn't have me, then no one could."

"Remind you of anyone?" Nesrin snarled.

"That's why we need your help." I reached out and brushed my fingers through hers. She was cold, like an icy breeze on my skin. "Salome's uncle is a lot like Brutus. Selfish. Vengeful. Power hungry. And those are the most dangerous kind of people."

We glanced over to Salome who remained quiet, her hands wrapped around her middle, and my heart bled for her. Being forced to marry a family member was horrific enough let alone the person who murdered your parents.

Nesrin reached out to her friend, taking her hand and drawing her into a hug. Salome's soft sobs were like a hammer to my chest. Ava pressed against my side, and my hand slipped into hers. We had each other, and sometimes that was all that mattered.

Cassidy made soft humming sounds; a familiar song, but I couldn't quite place it. Probably something from the eighties.

When Salome wiped her eyes and pulled away from Nesrin, she looked over to Cassidy who was curling her hair around a finger and pretending to be blowing bubble gum.

"Is Arson wandering the grounds too?"

Cassidy hopped off the wooden crate and dropped the shackles from her grip. "Haven't seen him. I tried to, for a long time. I tried to say how sorry I was, but he never came here...he never came to see me again. I searched and searched and searched. I figured maybe he didn't want to see me." Her face twisted into a mask of sadness. "But if he's here, he'll be at the seat."

"Where's that?" I asked, already taking a step toward the door.

"It's a place he went to be on his own. A place where he could...be himself. He went there alone mostly, or with Sebastian."

"Where is this seat? Can you tell us."

"I can do better than that." Cassidy shoved up from the floor in one ghostly slide and hovered with her feet an inch from the ground. "I can show you."

She turned, took one glance at the others and drifted along the landing, and then in a whisper of air she was gone.

"Hey!" Ava called out as I hurried after the ghost. "We can't walk through walls!"

Nesrin gave a snarl, and then barged past, careening down the stairs. "She'll be outside. This way."

A light breeze ruffled my skirt as I pushed through the dorm doors and rushed outside. But she was already floating along the footpath, slipping away from us.

Ava sucked in hard breaths beside me and lifted a hand. "How the Hell did she get so far?"

Cassidy was skipping along the lawn, heading straight for the woods behind Chuck's place, her head bopping to some song only she could hear.

The pond and church lay in the opposite direction. This woodland seemed dense and flooded with shadows.

"Heard this part of the forest is haunted," Nesrin murmured as we chased after Cassidy, who slipped past Chuck's cottage and made a beeline for the woods.

"More haunted than the Academy?" I almost choked on my laughter.

Nesrin smiled, and there was something calming about seeing her happy as opposed to always frowning or glaring at me. "You have a point."

Ava looked at me with worry darkening her gaze. "Do you think Chuck's in trouble? There was so much blood, you know."

"If anyone can take care of themselves, it's Chuck. And he didn't look worried."

"I suppose." She looked back at the cottage, and while I didn't voice it, the notion had crossed my mind too. I never asked what Chuck did for my dad. Well aside from guard duty. But the fact he'd brought some of that business to campus left me curious.

"Where's Cassidy?" Nesrin growled.

I snapped my attention to the woods, huffing. "Where the hell is she?"

"*Cassidy!*" Ava cried out.

A light whistle floated on the wind from directly ahead of us, and we all broke into a sprint, bursting into the woods. We leapt over dead branches and ducked under low hanging ones. A strong timber scent engulfed my senses, along with fresh soil. Shadows shifted around us like dancing spirits, and a shiver raced down my arms.

That familiar hummed tune came to me from the right, and combined with the lingering scent of hairspray made me turn. "She's this way." I pushed past a shrub that snagged on my skirt, and covered my long socks with tiny needles.

Ava was screeching as she kicked and tore at the shrub that she'd got caught in. "My foot's stuck."

I rushed back and tore the damn plant out of the ground, roots and all, unhooking the branch that had tangled around her shoe.

"And you are free." I tossed the damn thing aside, noting she was also covered in the tiny thorny needles.

We turned to Nesrin and Salome, who'd been smart

enough to go around the shrubs, unlike us, who marched right through them. I turned and hurried around the plants. It wasn't long before we found Cassidy, leaning against a huge oak tree, its branches like an umbrella around her, and leaves so bright green they might as well be emeralds.

"Wow," Salome mumbled.

"Took you long enough," Cassidy teased.

"Well, if you hadn't noticed, we can't walk through walls," Ava snapped back, huffing, and plucking the tiny needles out of her socks.

Cassidy's face fell, and she lowered her gaze, capturing Ava's attention.

"Look, I didn't mean it that way." My bestie moved toward Cassidy. "It sucks what Brutus did to you. Sorry."

Cassidy tilted her chin up and shrugged. "You probably should avoid the shrubs. Those things attack."

"Yeah, we worked that out the hard way," Ava murmured.

"So, where's Arson?" I scanned the woods around us, finding no sign of him.

"Look up," was all Cassidy said, and so we did. "Can you see him there? It's where he used to sit. I can't see him...can't see anything but a damn empty tree."

A pair of dangling legs swung from a branch and looking down at us was Arson. Shaggy, sandy hair fell around his strong face, with a light golden shadow of growth stretching over his jawline. Those eyes, amber pebbles, met mine, and behind them lay so much sadness. He'd been brought back as a ghost only to be reminded of the life he'd lost. I couldn't imagine how that must feel.

"He's there."

Pain crowded her eyes. She gave a weak smile. "Good, I'm glad he's there, but if you wanna talk to him, you'll have to climb the tree." She strolled several feet away and kicked at the foliage, but her foot just traveled right through the dried leaves and twigs.

"I'll do it," Salome piped up, before anyone could respond. Nesrin locked her fingers together, lowering her hands for Salome, who stepped up. She leapt, her hands grasping the lowest branch, pulling herself up with the ease of a gymnast, and swinging her legs up and over the branch.

All I saw were long legs and black underwear. In three graceful moves, she was balanced on the branch and inched around the trunk to reach Arson on the opposite side.

I shifted nervously, watching as I stood with the others.

Salome's soft whispers reached us, but I couldn't make out the words.

"So, is Cyndi Lauper still killing it on the charts?" Cassidy asked.

"Nah. But her songs are classics," Ava explained. "I think I have some on one of my Spotify playlists."

"A what?" Cassidy's brow pulled together, and Ava went into an explanation of today's music, while Nesrin kept staring toward the tree, concern on her face.

The branch creaked as Salome dropped through the air, landing hard on the ground with a *thud*.

She strolled toward us, her expression tight and breaths deep. A deep etch of pain pulled the corners of her mouth down. "It's not going to work, forget it."

Nesrin was shaking her head and approached her friend. "What do you mean it's not going to work? He's right there." She threw her hand into the air toward the tree.

"Did he say no?" I added.

"I said, just forget it." Her shoulders dropped in a defeat, and I hated seeing her this way. "I'm not doing this. Not using someone like that."

We'd come this far and there was no way we were giving up now. "There has to be something he needs or wants," I suggested. "Everything is negotiable."

"Like Hell you aren't." Nesrin growled, and reached out, grabbing her arm. "We don't give up, you hear me. Not when we have a way to get you out of this. *We never give up,*"

Tears shone in Salome's eyes as Nesrin dropped her hand and then marched toward the tree. I followed Nesrin with my heart in the back of my throat.

If I thought Salome made scaling the tree look easy, then Nesrin seemed to walk on damn air. One powerful lunge and she grasped the branch above her and kicked off the trunk to land on the thick branch where Arson sat. "What did you say to her?"

He'd watched her the entire time, following her movements, but he never turned to her, just answered. "She asked me if I liked the view. I told her I don't see a view. I don't see anything. All I hear is voices, all I feel is being stuck. It's like I'm between two walls, trapped."

Nesrin didn't respond right away but sat down on the branch next to him, her hard expression softening. With a deep inhale she twisted to face the spirit and studied him as if seeing him for the first time.

"I once had this friend," she began. "Well, I thought she was someone I could trust, but she wasn't really a friend."

Arson turned to face her. The faint honeyed glow of his aura brightened. I could see the need to connect to someone written on his face as he listened to the Panther.

"She did some shitty things, I'm not gonna lie. And for a while there...I did them too. I thought she was a friend. I thought she was someone I could confide in. Someone I could trust. But the truth was, deep down, I knew what she really was, but I didn't want to be alone."

Arson nodded. "Sometimes it's easier to turn a blind eye."

"I see that now, and I also see that during that time, it allowed the space for another friend of mine to shine." Nesrin glanced over to where Salome stood.

"It was the same with me," Arson murmured, "I fell in love standing under this tree, and I fell hard."

I watched them, like they'd known each other before. It didn't matter what they said, but that they said it. That they talked and connected in a way I didn't think I could.

I didn't think Nesrin had this side to her.

"You know what it feels like," she continued. "When a friendship takes a hard right turn and starts to feel a little like love."

I blinked hard. Had I heard right? Found love. With Salome? Like friendship love? I glanced to Ava. I loved the weird, pain in the ass. But when Nesrin looked at Salome, it was different. Now that I thought about it, her stare was the same way I looked at the Wolves.

Arson was captivated with Nesrin's company as she started to tell him the reason why we needed him.

"So, Mor here has this crazy idea she can somehow bring you closer to life. And I'm asking you...*no,* I'm begging you. Will you help us?"

I didn't dare move. The words playing over and over in my head. *Please say yes, please.*

"For love?" Arson murmured, and lifted his gaze to Salome, and then found Cassidy. "Yes, I'll try for love."

# CHAPTER SIXTEEN

## HIDDEN DISCOVERIES

Sunset came and went. All of us took turns pacing the floor, eventually finding ourselves pulling back the blinds at the front of Chuck's cottage to peer outside.

"Did he say when he'd be here?" Judas turned to glance over his shoulder.

I just shook my head. "For the tenth time, no. He just said he'd be here. We have to wait."

"I hate waiting," Nesrin snarled. "I should have specified a time."

"I doubt ghosts follow the clock," Ava added. "I think they just pop in and out when they feel like it."

"More coffee?" Chuck shoved from the sofa to stand.

I shook my head, and my stomach clenched. Acid welled in my belly, sloshing as I moved. I had to move. I had to keep walking, keep being busy...keep doing anything, as long as it wasn't staring at that damn window.

Night was closing in. Through the slats in the blinds, deep pink skies were turning red. It was a bad sign...I just knew it. I turned to the doorway. "Maybe I should—"

Nesrin stiffened, her gaze focusing on the doorway as

Salome stopped pacing behind her. Through the gaps in the door came a golden yellow light. It spilled around the doorframe, and then through the wood as Arson Arlo stepped into the middle of the cottage.

The Wolves fell silent.

Chuck's hands twitched at his sides.

Every one of us stared at the yellow haired ghost as he lifted his gaze to Salome.

"Thank you," she murmured and stepped forward. "I know we're asking a lot of you."

He just nodded and glanced to Judas. "Wolf."

"Lion," Judas returned, his voice deep.

Alpha to Alpha, the two eyed each other, but there was no tension in the room...just respect.

"I want to say thank you for doing this," Judas started, unsure where to look as the golden light ebbed and flowed around Arson.

"I don't know how to help, but I'll try," Arson murmured, his gaze sweeping across the room at all the eyes on him.

If he was nervous, it didn't show. He was an Alpha and just like Judas, they knew how to convey the strong leader image to others.

"Come in," Nesrin broke the silence. "There's a seat. Hmm... or hover? Sorry, haven't had many spirit visitors."

She was nervous. We were all nervous. Careful glances. The Wolves watched his every move. Muscles flexed as he strode forward.

Judas flopped onto the opposite couch, mimicking the Lion's every move. Must be some Alpha thing.

Chuck pulled up a chair from the table, while Jubba darted into the room and unleashed a hiss.

"Come here, you." Ava scooped him into her arms and sat back down.

"I'd ask if you wanted coffee," Chuck began, staring at Arson. "But..." He shrugged.

"Don't like the stuff." He shook his head and earned a wince from Ava. Then again, she guzzled the stuff like nobody's business.

"I'm here." He met every gaze. "So, what do you need me to do?"

Everyone in the room turned to me.

"Basically, I need to see if I can summon you into existence." I answered not just him, but myself. *Existence.* I stared at his glowing light, trying to figure out how that might feel.

"Sounds easy," he said with a flicker of a smile.

A hard bark of laughter tore from my lips.

Judas laid his hand on my thigh. Fingers skimmed my skin as he looked into my eyes. "I believe in you."

The weight of it all was so heady. What if's crowded inside my head, making me shove up from the sofa, needing space.

I paced the floor. "It's not really. I mean. I don't know if I can do this. I don't know if the power that made the Witch storm possible is still inside me."

"Then we try with what we have." Salome answered for everyone.

*And if we can't....*

The words rattled inside my head. It was only her life at stake here, right?

Only a marriage to a foul, murderous sonofabitch. I gave a nod. "Then we try. We try and we keep trying until we find a way."

I pushed aside all thoughts, and closed my eyes.

*And called to my power.*

The first faint flickers of energy rose to my call, growing stronger the deeper I sank into the well inside me. I lifted my hand, pressed my fingers to the middle of my chest as the entire room fell silent. I could feel their gazes, feel their energy...feel *everything*. Their power hummed and buzzed inside my head. Chuck was cold and hard, his outline jagged and sharp, and when I touched him in my mind, it stung,

I opened my eyes and carried a chair before sitting in front of Arson. "Okay, let's try this."

He sat unmoving, so I closed my eyes, reaching down deep, searching for my power. I didn't fully understand, but I embraced it as part of me.

I imagined a current of power curling from my body and around Arson's, injecting him with electric magic. *Come back to life.*

With little idea how I'd even brought about the Witch Storm or how I resurrected Principal Stone, I had to do it again. I had to make this happen for Salome's sake. So, I dug deeper to find my true magic.

Power tingled beneath the surface, pushing down on me like a giant hand, but I pulled at it as if it were taffy, stretching and slipping out of my grasp.

Arson groaned.

I opened my eyes and wobbled on my seat. A golden hue shimmered around Arson as if he might be glowing from the inside out, his chest heaving with each breath. In and out.

"I think it's working," Ava called out.

The ability simmered beneath my skin like a bubbling cauldron, and I pushed the invisible power at Arson, driving it into him. The room suddenly tilted around me as I started falling off the chair, but Judas leapt to my side, catching me, and bringing me back upright.

"I've got you," he mumbled, his strong hands holding me. Nero was on my other side, also kneeling, keeping me in place.

I used their arms, holding onto them, and kept focusing on drawing my power. My body was riddled with energy, skipping down my arms and back.

A smell hit my nostrils. Something old like it'd been closed up in a closet for years. No... it was so much more because it slithered up my body, icy, and left me trembling.

I sniffed the air, leaning closer to Judas but the scent faded, so I moved toward to Nero, and he hummed with this new energy that would steal my breath if I had any. Whatever I sensed felt strong... dangerous.

"Everything alright?" he asked, eyeing me strangely.

The scent of whatever came from him grew stronger, fiercer, and it tore me from my power, which curled up and vanished. I couldn't stop the tears bubbling in my eyes as fear surged through me and rattled me to the core. I didn't recognize his power as it shivered over my flesh.

"Shit!" I mumbled and swayed in their arms, my body exhausted, before collapsing against Judas.

"It's not enough," he explained as he held me. "You're hurting yourself."

I liked the way he smelled... all timbery and fresh and sexy. My vision danced as I glanced over to Nero whose brow furrowed with confusion, except there was something going on with him. I couldn't work it out why he smelled so... different... so dangerous. Something was wrong with him.

"Mor." Arson leaned closer, his body radiating light like

a bulb, but it wasn't enough because he was still transparent, still a ghost...

"Are you okay? Maybe it's too much for you," Nero suggested.

I shook my head, pushing him and Judas away, standing on my own. "It's not. I can do this."

Ava took my hand in hers. "We'll try again, but you need to rest first."

I met Salome's gaze, an ache settling under my heart that I'd let her down. Disappointment washed through me.

"I can definitely feel my body... but I feel different," Arson interrupted us, and I looked at him, studied the way the glowing aura remained, just needing a zap more power, something to make the transition of his change.

Arson reached for his mouth, his lips parted but instead of thick carnivore fangs, his teeth were thin, pointed. He rubbed his chest. "I can't sense my heart...almost like I'm a—"

"Vampire," Judas answered for him.

"You're pouring your power into him, Mor, but that's not the power he needs," Chuck murmured.

Arson looked over to Chuck, when Nesrin added, "He needs his own kind."

Salome swallowed hard and glanced to Nesrin. "I don't think I can."

"You can do it. When you transform into your lion, your energy will be the greatest and Mor can draw on it."

"And then?" Panic surged, making her words tremble. "Plus, I don't want to change in front of everyone."

Nesrin sighed and scanned the room, staring at each of us. "We do this together, draw on all our energies. How about that?" Her gaze swept over to mine. "Will that work, can you do it, say...if we're in there?" She motioned to the bedroom down the hallway and looked at me. "Can you draw on our energies from that room?"

I shrugged. "I can try."

Everyone made sounds of agreement, but uncertainty had settled on our shoulders.

"I'm ready to try whatever it takes," I murmured and stepped past Judas and into the hallway. "You okay with this, Chuck?"

"As long as she doesn't use the bed as a scratching pole, go for it." Ava glared at him, and Chuck laughed. "Right, Jubba's already chewed and scratched everything in this place."

Salome climbed to her feet and stepped past everyone in the room, the corner of her mouth curling at Chuck's attempt at a joke.

"Thanks," Arson muttered, and Salome met his gaze. She smiled, as though they'd communicated something wordlessly, and then walked faster, her shoulders squared.

I opened the bedroom door for Salome when Nesrin squeezed in past me. "I'll stay with her." She looked at me, almost pleading me to understand.

"Of course." If Ava was upset and worried, I'd be by her side if she shifted... heck, I'd seen her transform and I had to step several feet away to avoid getting slapped by her tentacles. I adored her for who she was, just as Nesrin did with Salome.

I shut the door, closing them inside, and turned toward the living room where everyone looked my way.

"So, what do we need to do?" Ava asked.

"Close your eyes, slow your breathing, and focus on a place that always brings you joy. I'll do the rest," I explained, hoping this worked, hoping Nesrin was right, hoping with all my might that we'd bring Arson into his real form. Deep inside, doubt swirled, but I shoved it aside, needing to believe that, somehow, I could do this.

"We're ready," Nesrin called from the bedroom.

I emptied my mind, thought of my calming place... the park Dad used to take me as a kid, wherehe'd teach me how to climb trees. Something about the place always eased me.

I stepped closer to the living room, finding Arson; his eyes were shut tight and he was burning bright, just like before. He was ready. We all were.

All thoughts dissolved as I called my power. The hairs on my arms shifted, and I felt that energy again, still there but weaker.

Arson shifted uncomfortably in his seat, so I reached out to everyone else's power. And they found me, curling around me like vines. The Lion-shifter twisted in his seat as if the energy wrapped him tight, squeezing and squeezing.

The further I pushed, the stronger our combined power rocked me at the core. It pricked my skin, feeling so different from when I'd been focusing on drawing just my own energy. Now mine was the thread that bound; it slipped in with everyone else's, tangling them together like a cobweb, connecting each one of us.

Arson unleashed a growl as his body was thrown backward against the seat, his head tilted back as he convulsed.

Ava shifted to help him, but I groaned and shook my head. Falling back next to Chuck, she continued her mediation, and with all of us humming, an enormous surge of electricity flooded through me. I could barely feel my body, but I held my sights locked on Arson, pummeling all my power into him.

*Please work. Please.*

His cries broke me, but when the first licks of a solid form crawled up his legs, a new explosion of adrenaline hit me. I inhaled everyone's power and it trembled through me, through all of us. I sensed more of it lurking just beneath the surface... Just out of reach.

Arson's limbs spasmed, and he rolled off the couch, hitting the floor with a thud. No one moved, no one dared.

Not now. Not while my inner battle made progress. I pushed so damn hard.

The Lion-shifter's mouth twisted into a snarl, his legs solid to his thighs, and that solidity climbed so slowly it drew on every inch of strength I had remaining.

His body glowed like the sun. I kept fighting, pushing and pulling. My legs shook beneath me, and I let the wall catch me before I slid to my ass, unable to hold myself upright.

The energy spiked as a result, sending a ripple through me, then sliced out from my body into the atmosphere like heat waves. My chest tightened and everyone cried out in a sudden explosive snap. They moaned and writhed about in anguish.

I couldn't keep going. My whole body was wracked with exhaustion. No matter how much I tried, I didn't have the strength to reach the power just out of grasp. I scrambled on hands and knees toward Arson to find his body's shimmer fading, and his solid legs fading before my eyes.

*No, no, no.*

My throat tightened. I couldn't do this no matter how much I tried. I'd failed.

Just like a flip of a switch, my power floundered and dissipated.

"What happened?" Arson muttered, pulling himself up from the floor, his gaze wild.

"I can't do this." I got up, and Bond rushed to my side,

his arm looped around my back, holding me close. "No matter how much I push, it's never enough."

"Maybe we're missing something?" Ava piped up, and I nodded, except I had no clue what the missing link was.

I staggered deeper into the living room, pressed up against Bond, my fists curled into balls because I wanted this to work, hoped it was the answer to helping Salome.

"I'm not strong enough." I admitted defeat, hating the sound of my deflated voice.

The door creaked behind me, and the tapping footfalls from Salome and Nesrin had me wanting to hide from the world.

I turned to them. "I'm sorry, Salome for letting you down."

"You didn't. We'll try something new," she murmured, but I heard the undertone to her words. Bone deep disappointment. Exactly how I felt.

I shook with a rising anger at myself. I pushed away from Bond and staggered to the table before snatching the folder. "Maybe I missed something. That must be it." I carried it into the living room when several aged photos of students and papers slid out and cascaded to my feet.

I bent down to pick them up, when Arson asked, "Why do you have a photo of Thorus in that folder?"

# CHAPTER SEVENTEEN

### SOFT IN THE HEAD

I TURNED MY HEAD. ARSON'S GAZE WAS FIXED ON THE image I'd just shoved to the side. "Thorus?"

"Yes," he murmured without meeting my gaze. "My lover."

I followed his focus to the faded class photo. They were the same kind of monsters...the same beautiful beasts we had now; pale-skinned Vampires, silver-eyed Wolves, towering thick outlines of a Ghoul in the back, and in the front the sickening too-wide smile of a Goblin. I scanned each face, moving from one to the other, and then froze.

The photo trembled, before I flinched and jerked my hand away.

I was moving before I realized, stepping backwards as the image floated to the floor, face down.

Voices crowded in, panicked gazes met mine, and lips moved as Judas took a step toward me moving in slow motion. But I couldn't hear what he was saying...only Arson's voice inside my head....

*My lover...My lover...My lover...*

The ghost bent down and skimmed phantom fingers over the image on the floor.

"What happened?" Panic filled Judas' eyes. "Talk to me."

Arson clawed the photo, desperately needing to see those midnight eyes from the man in the second row once more. But I didn't want to see them again...ever.

"It's his lover..." I whispered as Nero bent next to the ghost and turned the class picture over.

"No fucking way," he murmured and then lifted his gaze to mine. "This fucking demon...he just won't stay away, will he?"

"It's Thorin." The words sounded hollow, just like my chest. "Arson's lover...is Thorin."

"How do you know him?" Arson took a careful step.

I could already see the wince in his eyes, already see the pain this was going to cause him. But to lie would hurt more. "I know him as Thorin Tala, a demon who came to work for my father about ten years ago. He started as a driver, and then worked his way up until he became important to my dad...and then started dating me."

There was a hiss of breath, a shake of his head. His ghostly glow brightened for a second, and then faded, stealing away his hold on this world until he slowly disappeared.

"No, that's not him," his faint words slipped into the room.

"I'm sorry, I'm so sorry." I murmured.

"He told me he loved me...told me I was the only one...."

Judas' face was a mask of cold, stony rage. Fists clenched by his side, breaths slow, and deep.

"He was the one behind the diamonds," I murmured, and

Arson's golden glow brightened the room. "He and a shifter, Brylee, sent another Vampire to leave me a bag of diamonds which were Dragon's Tears, a powerful conduit to syphon Vampire powers, almost killing an Ancient...and my family."

"The Witch storm?" Arson murmured, growing brighter and bolder.

"That was me." I lowered my gaze to the photo. "But it all started with him."

"Goddamn bastard," the ghost snarled. "I'd hurt him if I could, tear those soulless eyes from his body."

"You'd have to get in line," Judas answered as he turned to the ghost.

"Did you see this?" Nero glanced at the photo again. "That sword he's holding. It's the same one you took from the church."

I didn't want to look at him, didn't want to see the same black eyes that haunted my dreams. But I glanced to the weapon standing upright in the corner and then stepped toward Nero.

It was the same weapon, same carving, same hilt. It meant something to him. I didn't know if I was happy that I'd taken something he cared about, or weirded out.

"Maybe there's something else there?" Nero lifted the image. "Something we missed."

I shuddered at the thought of going back to the church basement, but one glance at the glistening sheen of tears on Salome's face told me what needed to be done. "It's okay," I answered. "I'll go on my own."

"Like Hell you will," Judas snarled.

"I'm going too." Ava stepped closer.

"I don't want to go." Nesrin stood, shoving the chair away from her. "We'll stay here, and try to figure this out."

"What about the booger? I mean Brutus," Ava murmured and glanced at the swords.

"The Vampire?" Arson growled and glowed like a golden neon light. "Is he still here?"

"I think he's trapped." Nesrin held out her hand for Salome as the Lion wiped her eyes and then stood. "I've heard of spirits like him. People who do terrible things, they get stuck to the same place they terrorized, they become..."

"Poltergeists." Ava shuddered with the name.

It felt like we'd turned full circle, back to the morning after the Witch storm had raged, back to Ava screaming and Poltergeists laughing. Back to chaos. Except this was different... we were no longer running scared, and we knew what was going on.

Arson stared past me, his brow furrowing, and sorrow caught in his gaze. It wasn't fair that those like him and Cassidy were still, after all these years, under the thumb of a vicious bully, and it killed me to see them going through this again.

"No way," I growled and strode across the living room and grasped the sword from against the wall. "I'm not letting this happen again. I'll find a way to put an end to it."

I closed my hand around the cold steel, and felt the hum as I heaved the weapon into the air. I didn't know why I'd taken this from the room under the church. Maybe there'd been some kind of connection I felt...or maybe I just wanted to hack stuff up.

But it felt good in my hands. It felt good to swing and cleave the air. It felt good not to be as scared...I was sick to death of feeling that way.

"Then let's do this." I met their gazes. Ava, Nesrin, and Salome; my friends, Chuck and Arson, the Wolves...*my lovers*. We'd fight whatever stood in our way.

Ava cut across the room, holding my gaze as she grabbed her sword and then headed for the door. Our footsteps echoed in the silence. There was nothing left to say.

We slipped through the night, heading for the place I hated most of all. Fear tightened my stomach and made my skin crawl. I clenched my grip on the sword at my side and shoved through the trees.

"I wonder if mortals have this much fun?" Ava murmured. "Striding through the trees, carrying heavy as fuck weapons, ready to cut me a slice of Poltergeist pie."

I wouldn't laugh...I wouldn't laugh....

"Make my serving with whipped cream," she snarled.

The steel blade hummed in my hand as we shoved through the last clump of trees and found ourselves at the edge of cemetery. The heady scent of fresh earth clung to the night air. Movement in the trees behind us made me jump and twist.

"Is she there?" Ava scanned the headstones.

"Is *who* there?" I looked around, uncertain who she was talking about. "Cassidy?"

"Stone," she muttered without meeting my gaze. "That's who you're looking for, right? *You* think Stone's gonna come back and bite you on the ass, and Balefire's gonna turn you into the council."

"What? I don't think that."

"Yes, you do, in fact you're secretly hoping for it." She took a step into the clearing and headed for the fallen down timber fence. "I see the way you throw yourself into danger. I think you want this to be over with, once and for all, and I haven't even started with Thorin."

The tip of her blade cut a line in the earth as she dragged it behind her. The others pushed through the trees behind me as I took a step and followed Ava between fallen down fencing to where the headstones waited.

I exchanged a long glance with Ava, unsure where her comment came from? Hell, I didn't want to be thrown to the council or face Stone, but I did rush at danger to help protect those around me. And what did she mean about Thorin?

Something scurried through the dark to my right, grabbing my attention. I flinched, jerking my gaze to the mound of dirt pushed from where we buried Stone. Maybe Ava was right, maybe I was done with the lying and the fear. Done with looking over my shoulder, terrified of losing...not my life...but my friends.

They never showed this part of friendship in 90210. There was no close up of exhausted, worried faces as they waited for *their* dead Principal to come for them. They'd never experienced as much drama as I had since starting at this Academy.

I lifted my head to the church and a shiver cut through me as Ava climbed the first stair.

"This is your time, Mor. Time to face your fears, time for this to be over with." She heaved the sword into the air. "Time to open the windows and doors, and get rid of the unwelcome goddamn guests."

A faint orange glow came from the sword in her hand. The more she talked, the brighter it became, like her energy traveled along the steel. I glanced down to my own, to the cold glint, the blade just waiting for the same kind of flare to come to life.

We left the cemetery behind and mounted the church's stairs behind her. I felt hollow and empty. I'd tried to bring Arson back to life, tried to share part of my soul, and my power.

But it hadn't worked.

All it did was leave me empty.

*And afraid.*

The green glow inside the church brightened as I stepped toward the open door.

"You wanted to be strong, you wanted to be powerful," Ava murmured beside me. "Then this is your time."

"It is my time." I clenched the hilt, and deep inside me a flicker of power answered the call.

There was hope, and while I had that to cling to, I was prepared to face the monster of my past. We stepped together, just like we'd done this whole journey. The hinges squealed as I shoved open the door and walked inside. The dance of power trembled through my fingers and hummed against the steel.

"Your sword," Ava whispered. "It's glowing."

"Just like yours," I answered and caught the movement as she looked at her own weapon.

"Holy freaking nut sack."

A sickening snigger came from the darkness. "You think you can carve your way to the truth, do you?"

Brutus balanced on one of the fallen pews, waiting for us. He was even fatter and grosser than I remembered. Beady eyes shone with excitement. I didn't know if I hated him more because of what he was or what he'd done.

One glance to the closed trap door in the middle of the church floor and he floated to the ground in front of me. "I'm going to enjoy this." He crossed his arms, bulging his belly like an overfilled balloon.

"So am I," came the low growl.

Arson slipped into the church behind me, stopping at my side to stare at his murderer. His soft golden glow sharpened, deep brown eyes sparkled with life. The kind I hadn't had the strength to give him earlier.

But he found it now, dressed in anger, cloaked with fear.

"Do you remember me, Brutus?" He took a step forward as long claws grew from the tips of his fingers. "Do you remember what you did to me...and Cassidy?"

"Cassidy?" The foul creature repeated.

There was a twitch of his face, like somehow he'd forgotten he'd murdered two people.

"You killed her." Arson's growl rumbled through the room. "You killed her because you couldn't have her...and then you killed me."

Brutus shook his head as the Wolves and Chuck moved into the church ahead of us.

"I didn't want to," the tortured soul whispered. "He was saying things, twisting things inside my head...making me want to..."

"Who was?" I took a step closer. "Who was saying this to you?"

"Thorus."

A chill slipped along my spine. I glanced to the closed hatch and gripped the sword. "You're saying Thorin...*I mean,* Thorus was making you do these things?"

"Once I started believing them, I just couldn't stop." The green glow dulled around him. "It just came over me, I was feeding and feeding and feeding."

"Because you're an Emotional Vampire," I answered. "But he knew that, didn't he? He knew it all, every bit of it."

I didn't need Brutus to answer, still he nodded his head. In an instant he seemed to change, gone was the green glow, gone was the *ugliness* about him. A pale white light replaced the harsh neon as he floated to the floor. "I didn't even love her," he answered. "I just knew that I needed to have her, and the fact she didn't want me, made me want her even more."

"Because you fed on her fear." I left the others behind. "And Thorin, the Demon-hearted piece of shit, was counting on it."

Footsteps echoed with mine, the sword beside me a strong orange beacon of light in the darkness. "If you think I'm letting you go down there alone, then you've gone soft in the head," Ava murmured.

I swung my sword, letting all my power race through my fingers and into the steel. Bright pink glinted from the blade and, for the first time in a long time, I smiled, remembering a hot pink skirt and tights. "This is for Cassidy," I growled.

"For all the ones left behind," Ava glanced at me. "Let's do this."

I stopped at the hatch door, bent to grasp the ring flattened to the floor, and yanked. One glance at Judas and I was bending to find the ladder. Fear echoed in my Alpha's brown eyes. He glanced into the hidden space under the floorboards, stepping closer. "Be careful," he whispered.

I was tired of being careful.

I was tired of running away and hiding from my problems.

I gripped the ladder and eased myself down into the hole. The pink light brightened my way as I let go, landing on the floor with a *thud*. Ava followed close behind. She carved the air with her sword, scanning the darkness.

"Something feels different down here." She took a step.

The cold seemed to reach through the earth to whisper *he's here...he's been here all this time.*

Beside me the room brightened to a soft golden glow as Arson moved towards us, looking around at the mess of cabinets and desks. The Wolves and Chuck followed close behind, but they didn't need to worry.

Thorin wasn't here.

"He's been here," Arson murmured, dragging his phantom touch through the papers that littered the desk. "All this time. I always wondered why he never came to see me. Not once, not even at the beginning."

An ache spilled from my chest at the sight. I stepped closer, lowering my sword to reach out and touch him. "I'm so sorry."

"Let's go through everything again." Chuck moved toward the first cabinet. "There must be something we can use here."

Drawers were yanked open, files were pulled free. Arson skimmed his fingers across the desk and then sat in the chair. There was longing all over his face. The Lion loved the Demon more than I ever could have. What little feeling I'd had for Thorin was now burning under a pit of rage.

"What the fuck," Judas whispered as he stood next to Arson, flipping open the folders. "These weren't here before."

The Alpha lifted his gaze, confusion mingled with fear as he clutched a black and white image. But it wasn't me he looked at...it was Bond.

"What is it?" I murmured.

Bond was already moving as Judas lifted the image.

"Isn't this your sister?" Judas murmured.

There was a shake of Bond's head, but his eyes were fixed on the girl in the middle of the image. "That's not her...that's not Evie. She's at home...she's at home."

He turned away then, moving slowly, and headed back

to an open cabinet. Judas just looked at the image and then shook his head. "Could've sworn..."

"Can I see that?" I reached for the image.

The cabinet drawer closed with a *boom!* Bond turned and strode past us. "I need some air."

He was gone in an instant, gripping the side of the ladder and kicking off the dirt walls to lunge through the opening. I glanced at Judas who lifted his gaze from the image and then gave a shrug.

"I'm sorry," the words came from behind me.

We all turned to see Brutus standing in the middle of the room, looking solemn and very different from the green glob he was before.

"Please, forgive me." He looked at Arson. "I didn't mean..." his words faded.

"Forgive you for murdering a woman who deserved it even less than I did?" Arson murmured, as he moved closer.

"You're right." Brutus hung his head. "I don't deserve your forgiveness. I should have seen the truth behind Thorin's intentions, but I let him blind me with affection."

I caught my breath and the sound echoed through the room.

"If what you say is true, then you were just as much a victim as we were." Kindness spilled from Arson's hand as he reached for the spirit. "How can I hold hatred toward you when you were tricked? I forgive you.."

"I do too."

I jerked toward the sound as Cassidy floated through dirt ceiling.

"I'm sorry for what he did to you." She glanced to Arson, and I knew without needing the words that he could finally see her too. "I forgive you."

*He's trapped,* Nesrin's voice echoed inside my head as

Brutus' spirit sucked in a hard breath and sighed. He closed his eyes and drifted upwards; light spilled from inside him. Soft, tender.

"Thank you," he whispered, and then he opened his eyes.

But they weren't bright and clear, they weren't filled with love and kindness.

They were as black as the Night and as the *snap* of chains echoed through the room, a chill cut right to my soul.

"Now, I'm free." His sadistic smile stretched wide. "Now, *I am free.*"

Turning green and bulbous...and even more disgusting than before, he disappeared

Hell, we'd made a mistake.

*"I can smell sadness...I can taste fear...I'M COMING FOR YOU. I'M COMING FOR ALL OF YOU."*

"Oh, shit," Ava whispered. "What the fuck did we do?"

"We released a monster," Judas answered.

I jerked my gaze to the opening as faces filled my mind. But I stopped at two of them. Two who were hurting...two who were gripped with fear. "Nesrin," I whispered.

"Salome," Ava said at the same time.

I lunged for the ladder at the same time as Ava. We'd unleashed a monster on Bestias Academy. Again.

But this time we knew exactly who they wanted.

# CHAPTER EIGHTEEN

## DARK TIMES

I PLUNGED THROUGH THE TREES FOLLOWING THE FAINT sound of laughter. My heart was thundering as my boots slammed to the ground. All of us ran. I ignored my fear, but a small surge of my power rose, swelling, pressing, suffocating me. I sensed Brutus' energy, and the closer we got to Chuck's cottage, the more I knew I was on the right track.

Dread hung heavily in the night, looping around me, invading my mind. Something felt different about his power. I sensed it more than I had before, and it curled over my skin like snakes. Except, rage bubbled in my chest because the monster was targeting my friends, and we'd all fallen for his pity trick.

*Stupid. Stupid. Stupid.*

The cottage was in sight, and we sped up. Their breaths huffed alongside me, footfalls thudding the grass, but Chuck and the Wolves were faster, silent, like experts in stalking the night.

Chuck thumped open his front door and disappeared inside, the Wolves on his heels.

I leapt in after them with Ava, all of us rushing into the living room.

Nesrin and Salome stood as we barged inside. "What's going on?" Nesrin cut a glare to each of us.

I shook my head, sucking in hard breaths. "Nothing, I just thought…" I stilled.

How on earth was I going to tell her I thought they were being attacked, by a great big…

"Hunk of snot," Ava snarled beside me, sucking in hard breaths. "That's what you were thinking, right? That it was a big, ugly, crusted booger."

I winced at the words, but yeah, that's exactly what I was thinking.

"Ooo." Salome pressed a hand to the middle of her chest and unleashed a thunderous burp.

"Whoa," Nero muttered and waved his hand in front of his face. "What the Hell did you eat?"

"I dunno, just coffee…and a stale packet of peanuts Nesrin found in the cupboard."

The Panther strode into the living room, and glanced at Chuck. "You really need to put some food in there, especially if we're going to be this kickass crew."

"Did anything strange happen in the last ten minutes," Ava murmured, looking from Salome to Nesrin. "Well, aside from Salome burping like a drunk sailor."

"Just flickering lights," Nesrin said. "And then you lunatics. Ava you're…" She pointed to Ava's chest.

I glanced to where she was pointing as Chuck walked through the living room, drawing her gaze. "Oh shit, sorry." Ava grabbed the side of her bra and heaved it back into place. "Not now, party tit." She gave Nesrin a smile. "She's a rebel this one, won't do what she's told."

"Why do I even bother?" The Panther just shook her head.

"I told you, you can't hold a good tit down. *Hey, big fella?*" she roared over her shoulder to Chuck.

There was a chuckle from the kitchen. But that uncomfortable feeling grew, like a cold breeze that slipped in to sink into my bones. Footsteps echoed as Judas and Nero strode toward me. Both Wolves looked toward the window.

"Mor..." Judas started, reaching for my hand. "Get behind me."

I followed his gaze as a shadow cut across the window. Another one followed, low, quiet...*beastly.*

*Thud...thud...thud...*heartbeats echoed in unison. The scent of male drifted underneath the door frame and into the room.

"Chuck, do you have any weapons?" Nero whispered.

But the Vampire was already moving, taking off his jacket and draping it across the back of the sofa. "I don't need them...I am the weapon.'

"Mor." Judas glanced at me. "It's not safe, get behind me."

"You know." Chuck turned to the Alpha. "I'm getting a little tired of watching you treat her like a child. You know who she is. You've seen what she can do, and yet you think you're the one who can shield her from what's out there?" He jerked his head towards the window. "She's been handling beasts far more dangerous than you her entire damn life. How about you show her a little respect, and let the woman decide for herself when she needs you."

Nero's lips parted, mouth agape as Chuck rolled up his sleeve and turned toward me.

"That's my Vampire," Ava whispered as a savage rolling growl breached the door.

"Salome," Kinraide called from outside. "I'm giving you one last opportunity, come with me. You don't belong in this place, and you don't belong with them. I don't want to have to hurt your friends, but I will if you make me."

I jerked my gaze to Salome and shook my head. "Don't..."

Her amber Lion eyes blazed with fury. Nesrin grasped her wrist, pinning her to the Panther's side. "You stay with me."

I jerked back to the door as Chuck closed the distance, stilling at my side. I looked at the rolled sleeves and then lifted my head to the steely gaze of a killer. He glanced at the middle of my chest and then my eyes. "You going to be okay? Not going to unleash another damn Witch storm, are you?"

I glanced to Judas, is that what was worrying him? That I was somehow *unhinged*, tearing the void between right and wrong apart every time I was angry. I tore my gaze from the Wolf. I thought after all we'd been through he'd be honest with me. "Yeah, I'm good."

"Take it easy on him, he's still learning," Chuck growled and strode toward the door.

"*Hey.*" Ava took a step. "Do not do anything stupid, Chuck."

He stilled, looked over his shoulder, and the eyes of a killer stared back at her. "Yes, my love."

He grabbed the dagger from his waist, opened the door and in an instant, he was gone.

"*What the fucking fuck!*" Ava snarled and lunged for the door.

*Boom!* The blast of a gunshot filled the air.

I leapt for the door, meeting Ava mid-air. Hands collided, and fingers clawed as a brutal *thud* hit the other side of the door. Chuck slumped inside as we wrenched the damn thing open, his shirt a tattered mess of blood and pellets.

Pale lips curled, and dark eyes glinted with a look I'd seen many times. He shoved from the ground in the doorway and rose to his feet.

Outside there were Lions. *A lot of Lions.* More than there were before, and in the middle of this pissed off Pride was Kinraide.

"That there's a warning shot," he snarled, standing next to a Lion with a shotgun aimed at Chuck. "You come at me again, Vampire. And see what happens."

A sickening snarl came from the right of the pack. Rolling muscles, wild yellow-haired manes. Amber eyes flicked to me, and then to Chuck as young males shifted into their beast form and stalked forward.

"I'll fucking come at you." Ava pushed forward, slipping between me and Chuck to stride forward.

A cold wind picked up out of nowhere, casting strands of her hair into the air. Fear gripped my stomach as I strode forward to stand at her side.

"You going to let the girls do the fighting for you, is that it?" The smug piece of shit just smirked and shook his head.

Movement came from behind me, Nesrin and Salome stopped on my left. The four of us stood there, four against ten fully grown Lions. It almost seemed like a waste of our time to get our uniforms dirty.

"We fight for each other, love is what holds us together. That concept might be a little over your head, Uncle."

The thick stench of male was choking, it was all I could smell, all I could taste.

"I'll say this once more." Chuck stopped at our side, looking down to finger the pellet holes in his shirt. "The only one leaving here is you...in pieces if you don't piss off."

One of the young Lions growled and stalked forward, head down, eyes focused on his kill.

Silver shone in the night as a stained-tip dagger flipped end over end through the air and lodged in the beast's flank.

A howl was followed with grunt. The Lion slowly dropped to the ground, turning its head to bite at the dagger.

"Now, that's poisoned...and your soldier there is dying. You've got two choices, leave and get him to a healer, or stay and get your ass kicked by these '*girls*' as you put it."

Kinraide curled his lips, and then glanced at his fallen soldier. The beast was howling, clawing at the dagger in his side as he slowly shifted into mortal form. Golden fur slipped away, to leave pinkened flesh torn and bleeding.

"Kinraide," the beta at his side cast a panicked gaze to the fallen and then to his leader.

But there was no turning of this tide, no undoing what had already been done. The Vampire guard at our side wasn't playing.

He never played and neither did we. "Leave here." I glanced to the howling male as he clenched his grip around the hilt and then screamed with agony.

Salome flinched at my side, taking a slow step toward the shifter. "He's dying." She glanced at her uncle and screamed, "Take him to get help."

Chuck plucked another blade from the sheath at his side. "I'd do what the Princess says if I were you."

Kinraide flinched at the words. He jerked his gaze to the screaming man on the ground. There were others around the man now. One knelt on the ground at his side, hand gripped around the hilt.

"Steady," the Lion warned as two more came to his aid.

They held the shifter down and yanked the blade free with a gut-wrenching *squelch*. But Kinraide wasn't looking anymore. He moved fast, grasping the shotgun and aimed it at Chuck. "Now!" he roared.

Shifters lunged in all directions and the gun blast shattered the air with a deafening *boom!* Tentacles shot out in an instant, as Ava let out a piercing scream and charged forward. She was unrelenting, filling the darkness with terror. I tore after her, and Kinraide lifted the weapon, taking aim...but it wasn't at Chuck this time.

It was at my best friend.

"Ava...*no!*" The words ripped free as Lions met Wolves mid-air.

The *crunch* of bodies filled my ears, but I couldn't look at them now. All I saw was the tips of tentacles lash the air as Ava raced across the cottage's yard and headed for the Lions.

*Boom!* The crack of a gunshot was a punch to my chest.

Ava screamed and then stumbled as the tip of a tentacle flew through the air behind her.

"Ava!" Chuck roared.

A dagger sailed past me, silver glinting in the dark before it whipped past Kinraide, skimming the side of his head. Blood welled and spilled over his ear.

The night was savage, filled with the gnash of teeth as the battle commenced.

Salome bounded ahead and lunged into the air with an unmerciful scream. She collided with Kinraide, then they hit the ground and rolled.

I punched my feet into the ground as a Lion turned on Ava and swung his fist. Another came from the side, and one more slipped in behind.

They were closing her in, cutting her off from the rest of

us for an easy kill. A Lion sailed backwards through the air and hit the ground with a crack as Ava spun, her face a mask of rage.

"Come on then!" she screamed.

But the Lions had no idea what part of her to watch. I lunged into the air, opened my arms, and crashed into the Lion at her back.

We hit the ground hard and I clamped my legs around his thighs and bit.

Warmth hit me with a splash. The heady rush of blood filled my mouth as I savaged the Lions neck. I spat the blood out of my mouth. But then claws gouged into my side. The pain was blinding, and I was torn away from my victim.

Amber eyes flared, burning into my soul as he wrenched a massive paw into the air. He was shifting as he moved, leaving behind his mask of a man, and turning into the beast.

*"Morwenna!"* Chuck screamed my name.

And everything slowed for me.

Life.

*Love.*

*"No!"* Judas was a blur, charging forward to slam into the Lion above me.

The sight shattered something in me. Judas smashed into the Lion, slashing with claws. There was no stopping him, in his mindless rage...and it was all for me.

*Boom!* The shotgun blast kicked through the air once more.

Salome slumped to the ground and then rolled onto her back as Kinraide shoved to stand.

My hands wouldn't work. Mind could comprehend.

The bitter stench of gunpowder filled my nose as

Kinraide stumbled to stand and swung the muzzle of the shotgun through the air, stilling on Judas.

But he couldn't see the danger coming for him. He could only hack and claw. Only hurt, and keep on hurting, without any thought to his own safety.

The muzzle glinted in the air. Hate-filled eyes focussed on the man I loved. I was lunging before I heard the blast rang out in the air. I was punched in the chest and stumbled in front of him.

Judas' eyes were wide, the whites shining like the moon overhead.

*"Stop this!"* Salome's screams filled my head.

I couldn't breathe. I couldn't think.

I could only stand there, trembling as I looked down. Dark, dangerous power lashed out, but this wasn't born from the Vampire side of me. This was all dark. All consuming.

*All Hekate.*

Her energy tore through me like a sonic boom to thunder through the air.

"Mor?" Judas just stood there, staring at my chest.

"I'm okay," I whispered, but my voice wasn't my own.

It was husky and raw, echoing from the pit of my stomach.

"No more." Salome pushed to stand from the ground.

She looked at every one of us, stilling on Nesrin on the ground. "Get off her!" The Lioness stumbled forward.

I turned then and took in all the blood, the hurt and the pain. Chuck's shirt hung in tatters, claw marks raked his chest. He shoved the Lion in his grip away from him on one savage motion.

Judas reached for me, pulling me close, touching the

center of my chest as though he couldn't quite believe I was unhurt. "You scared me," he murmured.

"He was going to shoot you." I watched Salome pull Nesrin from the ground and then turn to her uncle. Nero was coming toward us, while Bond... He left the battlefield, hurrying somewhere else. Where was he going?

"Enough," Salome growled. "I can't do this. I can't stand by and watch you hurt them...not because of me."

"No, Salome." Nesrin took a step forward, but her knee gave way. She fell to the ground, but this time she stayed there.

"I'm sorry." Salome turned to her uncle. But her words were for us. "This is the only way. He'll never stop...never, ever."

Just like a change of the tide, the Lions dropped bloodied fists, and turned away from us.

And together with Salome they headed to their leader.

*Kinraide.*

# CHAPTER NINETEEN

## FALLEN

THE TREES SWAYED IN THE DISTANCE, STILL I STARED AT the place where Salome had disappeared into the night.

Nesrin whimpered and slammed her fist into the ground. *"Salome! Come back to me!"* Tears shone in her eyes. *"Salome!"*

Pain beat its own drum inside my chest.

It was all I could feel...hopelessness...*outrage.*

"No." Nesrin limped towards where we'd last seen Salome, her eyes slammed closed, features contorting with pain. "This isn't happening. No fucking way... I'm not letting her marry that monster."

"What choice does she have?" Nero murmured.

*"She has to have a choice here!"* Nesrin stumbled toward him, her eyes wide with rage and then swayed under the weight as shock closed in. "She has to a have choice...doesn't she?" She looked to the trees where Salome had disappeared. "She has to have a choice."

I clenched my fists and stumbled forward.

"I'm going after her," Judas growled behind me. "Nero..."

"I'm in." Nero answered.

"That's the smartest thing you've said yet, Wolf," Chuck muttered and strode forward, giving him a pat on the shoulder as he passed. "Looks like you're learning."

Nesrin stumbled forward, limping...but there were no whimpers, no cries for help. Instead she ground her jaw as we all followed, slipping through the same trees Salome had left behind minutes before.

I didn't know where we were headed, all I could do was follow the trail of desperation Salome had left behind. The longer we walked, the less Nesrin limped. She was healing fast. We were all healing.

Stars sparkled in the distance as the forest floor rose. I turned to glance over my shoulder to the sparkling lights of Bestias Academy far behind.

"Where the Hell are they going?" Ava swung a hand up, swiping a branch aside.

A mountain rose in the distance, the outline dark and looming.

"I bet that's where." Nesrin sucked in hard breaths.

Faint yellow lights flickered through the trees up ahead as the musky scent of Lion grew stronger.

"It's a cavern," Nero called over his shoulder.

"Of course, it is." Nesrin stumbled forward and grasped a low branch. "One way in and one way out. The bastard has to control everything she does."

"We still have no way of getting her out of there." Nero shook his head. "We can fight these guys all day long. We might win...and then again we might not."

I'd fight them...and I'd keep fighting, if that's what it took.

I glanced to Judas, but the thought of seeing him hurt like that killed me.

Up ahead, past the curtain of trees, the cavern's opening came into view, along with six lion-shifter guards flanking the entrance.

"I'll get you inside," Chuck growled and shoved forward.

I heard the thud of his steps for a second, and then he was gone, like a ghost in the night.

*Arson....*

His name filled me. I turned my head to the mass of trees at our back. Where the hell had he gotten to? Was this battle not important enough, kind of thing?

He was gone...*just like Bond had left after the fight.*

That stung.

A guard stepped away from the golden glow of the cavern entrance and lifted his head. The shotgun rested on his shoulder. Fingers quick to find the trigger. He was looking right at us...coming closer.

Until a blur of black snatched him away.

Trees rustled to the right, but there was nothing left of the guards...or their weapons.

"Let's go before another takes their place." Nero pushed forward, leading the way. Judas followed his Beta, glancing along the tree line before they cut across the clearing outside the gaping jaws of the mountain.

Voices echoed inside, deep snarls from Kinraide.

"It's started." Nesrin choked back a whimper and turned to me. "The bastard couldn't let her have a goddamn second."

"No..." I whispered as Nesrin pushed ahead, barely limping with her wounded knee.

Chuck strode in out of nowhere, slipping behind Judas and Nero as they stepped into the cavern. It was all I focused on, all that drove me as I left the cover of the tree-line behind.

Ava was first, slipping into the mountain and then Nesrin.

I swept my gaze left and right, finding and following the flickering light of torches deeper into the cave. The stench of still water and fire stung my nostrils, but I knew exactly why the prick had wanted Salome here. Why he chose this place for his hellish ceremony.

Control.

He kept her under his command, stopped her from running if she wanted. Except she wouldn't. Now that she was beaten.

The thought of that raged through me.

Our footsteps echoed like rapid gunfire as we emerged into a large cavern. Torches encircled a barren cave. Half a dozen lion-shifters stood at one end.

But my gaze fell onto Salome. And I gasped, tears stinging my eyes.

She was on hands and knees, crawling along the floor on her belly...as low as possible.

Nesrin moaned and her steps stilled, seized by the sight.

Salome's golden hair hung down, covering her face.

"Grovel," Kinraide commanded and lifted his cruel eyes to us.

Muffled words slipped from Salome. I couldn't hear the words. But I didn't need to.

Kinraide's lips curled into a smirk as Salome crawled closer. Still the piece of shit watched us and waved several guards closer to us.

Nesrin started forward, but I grabbed her arm. "Stop," I whispered.

Salome never looked at us, never once turned her head,

but kept low, crawling like she was nothing—and to him, she was. *No,* she was less than nothing.

"I can't..." Nesrin shook her head. "I can't allow this."

"Can't we do something?" Ava murmured.

"Pride Law remember." Those words had never felt so foul in my mouth. "We stop it, and we'll have the supernatural council after us, along with every Lion-shifter."

Salome stopped at her uncle's feet, waiting for the command to rise.

Instead he just held out his hand. "Give me the Chalotite stone, Salome."

I flinched at his demand and Salome mumbled words I couldn't quite make out.

"Speak up," he growled.

She lifted her head then. Lips curled, eyes sparkling with defiance. "I don't have it."

Kinraide's eyes locked on his niece, and then bent toward her. But Salome never moved, like somehow, she knew what was coming. *And she was ready for it.*

He snatched a handful of her hair and wrenched her head back, yanking until she had no choice but to climb to her feet.

She cried out, her spine bowing backwards, yielding under his cruel hand.

"Goddamn bastard." Chuck took a step forward.

*"You...DO NOT MOVE."* Kinraide wrenched his gaze to the Vampire warrior.

He yanked her hair harder, strands pulling the skin at the corners of her eyes until tears slipped free.

"The stone." He leaned closer. Amber eyes shimmered. The more furious he became, the closer to his Lion he got. "Where is it?"

Her hands trembled in the air, clawing his hands in a

desperate attempt to ease his hold. "I didn't bring it...I'm sorry. *Please, Kinraide. I'm sorry.*"

"*Stop it,*" Nesrin snarled, her skin darkened, eyes turned nice and round. The tips of long white fangs slipped over pale lips.

She was shifting...letting her beast take control. But with the animal side of herself...came her powerful, unstoppable rage.

The hairs rose along my arms, flesh prickling as she took a step forward.

"Leash that *bitch now,*" Kinraide roared.

Savage breaths only made the beast rise higher in Nesrin's gaze. Her fingers curled, long claws slipping the sheath of her nails.

But Kinraide released his grip just a little, leaving Salome trembling. "Get this done." He commanded. With a glance at the Lion at his side, he barked, "Start the ceremony."

Fat tears rolled down her cheeks, fear etched on her sorrowful expression. She winced, her hands grabbing for her hair to stop the pain. Her mouth opened, but her chin only quivered.

"Speak!" He pulled hard.

"*Stop this!*" I took a step forward.

Nesrin screamed with a desperation that cut through me. "*Leave her the fuck alone.*"

One of the guards came for her, pistol drawn, aimed at her chest. But she was ready, stepping back and to the side. Rage filled her eyes. "Come on," she growled. "Big man with a gun, aren't you?"

The Lion smiled as he watched her and then carefully tucked the gun into the waistband of his jeans.

Chuck moved at the same time as Nero, both men cutting off the Lion.

"You go for her, and you're gonna need to come through us."

"I want this over with now!" Kinraide grasped Salome's chin, forcing her to face him. "Now, say the goddamn words, before I make you say them."

She shuddered at his touch. "I...I..." Her words faded to a whisper, and I couldn't hear anything.

Kinraide tightened his grip, driving the soft flesh of her cheek against her teeth.

Blood slipped from her lips, running over pale flesh as she stared into his eyes.

"Louder," he roared. "Say it again. Let them hear how you pledge yourself to me."

She tried to swallow and then twitched. Her arms jolted, face contorting.

"Stop that." Kinraide pinched her face tighter.

But she couldn't stop. Instead she only grew worse, twitching and jumping.

"I...." she whimpered. "I *g-g-give m-m-mmyself...*"

Kinraide dropped his hold and took a step backwards, his gaze riveted to his bride to be as she jittered and jolted.

She tilted her chin high. "I'll obey you in all t—" And then with a sudden twitch, she stilled. Silent. Eyes unfocused...until with an inhuman roar she raged. "A...a...a...ll t...hi...ngs!"

"What the fuck?" Ava murmured.

*"Y...You."* She whipped her gaze to Kinraide. *"I WILL OBEY..."*

That was *not* Salome. Not this voice, not the sadistic gleam in her eyes.

But she was battling. Fighting something inside her.

Something that was trying desperately to get out.

"*YOU ARE ALPHA*," she panted, hands fisted at her side. A sheen of sweat shone across her brow, the bead of blood slipped over her lips and dripped to the floor.

"What the fuck is wrong with her?" Ava glanced to me.

"And I..." Salome snorted and slobbered on herself, her body shuddering, bones cracking.

"Is this a fucking joke?" her uncle roared. "Maybe she's too broken." The asshole barked a laugh. "Well, that makes things a lot easier, then doesn't it."

"Maybe she's in shock," I said as her eyes rolled into the back of her head.

"Fucking ghostbusters," Ava blurted. "She's damn possessed. Next thing, the fridge demon will come out."

I wrenched my gaze toward her, as Ava stilled for a second and then stared into my eyes as we spoke in unison. "*Brutus!*"

I jerked my gaze to Salome as she twitched and fought. He was there in the manic gleam of her eyes. Fighting for control. But Kinraide wasn't having anything to do with this, taking a step away.

"What the fuck did you do to her?" he screamed at us. "You broke her!"

Nesrin took a step closer, and smiled. "I'd rather she be broken than be with you."

But Kinraide wasn't done. He forced himself to move, taking a step to grasp Salome's arm. "This doesn't change a damn thing." He jerked his gaze toward a guard. "Get the goddamn cuffs. I'll punish the bitch if she won't heel."

"*No!*" Nesrin lunged, slamming her boots into the ground, stepping around Chuck and Nero before she leapt.

She was shifting, pale skin changing to shimmering black fur. She moved fast, more agile than anything I've ever seen before. She lowered her head, and charged as the Lion reached for a heavy set of shackles.

She hit the guard with a *crunch*. Yellow hair and black fur went flying. The shackles were tossed into the air and landed a foot away.

"Stop!" a roar came from behind us. "Stop the ceremony!"

*"What now?"* Kindraide snarled.

I spun and then winced at the glaring golden glow which pulsed, filling the cavern. I lifted my hand, shielding my eyes.

The closer the voice came the brighter the glow.

But I knew that voice. Inside my head a whisper cut through...*please help her*.

"Who the fuck are you?" Kinraide barked.

But the glowing orb only grew stronger, sharpening around his body as Arson stepped closer.

"My name is Arson Arlo and I have the Chalotite stone." He lifted his hand and unfurled his fingers. "And I'm commanding you to stop this ceremony...and let Salome go."

# CHAPTER TWENTY

### THE TURN OF THE PRIDE

"Arson Arlo?" Kinraide muttered as the glowing Lion strode past us.

He turned his head, and deep amber eyes met mine. There was a slow nod, just a tilt of his head in acknowledgement before he strode past. "I come from the Arlo Pride...the most powerful—"

"I know who you are," Kinraide snarled, and then glanced to Salome. "What I don't know is why the fuck you're here."

"Salome has promised herself to me."

"Like Hell she has." Nesrin shoved herself from the ground, clearly forgetting our earlier plan.

"Nesrin," I called her name, drawing her gaze. One shake of my head was all that was needed.

Couldn't she see this was Salome's only way out of this? She could be married to either a murderer, or a ghost. The Panther cut a glare to Arlo, her features softening as she turned to Salome once more.

"This doesn't concern you." Kinraide took a step, motioning the others of his pack forward with him.

"Besides, you're dead right? What good is a dead leader? May as well have followed the Salome's father, the previous King for the rest of their miserable lives if it came to that."

The Lion next to him gave a wince. He didn't like that...no, he didn't like that at all. Arson's outline sharpened as he glanced from the Lion at Kinraide's side to the scumbag himself. It looked like I wasn't the only one who'd noticed that.

"Salome's father was a respected leader of his tribe," the young Alpha spoke carefully, lifting the glowing stone in his hand. "Legend has it this stone burns bright for the true leader of the Pride. Tell me, Kinraide, does the stone come alive for you?"

Panic crowded the cruel Lion's eyes. He glanced at the glowing stone, pulsing with energy, brimming with life. Truth lingered in the silence.

"That's what I thought," Arson murmured.

"I don't need the stone," Kinraide snarled and then wrenched his gaze from Arson's outstretched hand to his eyes. "Not when I have her."

He moved fast, lunging to knock his guard out of the way. But Nesrin was moving, lunging with rippling muscles toward him.

Desperation drove Kinraide. He scrambled for purchase, grasping Salome as she twitched and shuddered, fighting the demon inside her in an effort to stand and fight. Kinraide's hand gripped her arm and he whipped her around, slamming her against the front of his body like a shield.

He dropped his hand to his waist and drew a thin, double edged dagger free, pressing it against her neck. "Come closer and I'll cut her."

Nesrin's voice was raw and hungry. "You touch her and I'll make you eat that fucking blade."

Kinraide never looked at her, only glanced over his shoulder and yanked Salome backwards. "I don't need the stone, not when I have the blood right here. They'll follow me, and if they won't...then they'll follow her."

Salome stumbled and jerked, dragging her boots along the dirt floor as Kinraide searched for a way out.

"You just going to let this piece of shit do this to her?" Nesrin turned on the Lions standing in the shadows. "She's your Princess, isn't she? Your Queen?"

One took a step forward, his gaze riveted on Kinraide, and Salome. "Maybe we should—"

*"No!"* Kinraide roared, and pressed the blade harder against her skin.

A single bead of red blood welled under the steel and slipped along her throat.

"That's enough," the Lion commanded. "We came to plead for a Queen...not kill one."

*"She is NOT YOUR QUEEN!"* Kinraide screamed. Veins pulsed at his temples, eyes stretched so wide I could see the whites. "I am *your King! ME...THAT'S ALL YOU HAVE...IS ME."*

"No." Salome stared at the Lion who had spoken out. "Julius, you pledged your life to my father, you honored us, cared for us. You...protected us."

"And you left...*us,*" he answered.

"Do you blame me?" she whispered. "If you were in my position, wouldn't you have done the same?"

"You don't belong here. You belong with your people."

"Then let me be with my people. Let me lead my people. I don't need a King to do that."

"Pride law..." he started and then glanced to Kinraide at her back.

"Pride law would see a monster on the throne, instead of someone who deserved to be there."

"I'll marry her." Arson held out the stone. "I'll marry and she can rule. If that's what it takes."

"And your children?" Julius glanced at Nesrin, and then to Salome. "We have no fighters, we have no warriors. We have nothing more than the scraps of a Pride, and the madness of a would be king."

"No, you'd have more than that." Arson stepped closer, his gaze on Salome. "If you wanted to, I'd pledge my blood-line, *my* Pride...*my family*."

A sudden gasp filled the cavern. Every Lion stared at Arson.

"He's lying," Kinraide snarled.

"You'd know," Salome murmured. "You've been doing it your entire life."

"You want a Queen and a Pride, or do you want someone like him, someone with no regard for bloodline, someone with no regard for you. He'll turn on you, just as he's turned on her."

Julius stared at the glowing stone in his hand. A stone that answered to the true call of an Alpha, a stone that was demanding to be seen.

"You're a ghost," Julius growled.

"And he's a murderer."

The answer was simple, and it shone in every set of amber eyes inside the cavern. The rest of the Pride moved, stepping closer...and lowering their weapons.

"Kinraide." Julius lifted his gaze to the sick sonofabitch. "Let her go."

Kinraide's brow furrowed as he glanced to his Beta and

then the rest of the pride. "No, you're not serious? You're not actually going to take a *fucking ghost* over me?"

"I won't say it again." Julius motioned his hand and the Pride moved in. "You wanted to stop her from escaping, but you didn't think about yourself."

Salome's fingers twitched at her side. Her gaze was locked with Nesrin's. There was a tiny shake of the Panther's head, big round eyes pleading.

But there was no stopping Salome, not when the woman she cared for was a foot away. Her hand rose swiftly and grasped Kinraide's hand around the blade, and with one sudden wrench of his hold, she twisted...snapping bone.

He flinched, trembled as the blade fell to the ground, and screamed. Chilling wails of agony resounded in the cavern as Salome turned on her captor, but it wasn't just Salome in there.

One eye twitched as she dragged her uncle forward, until his knees buckled and he crashed to the ground.

"Enough!" he howled. "I said *enough.*"

"But is it?" She stared down at him. "I don't think it is. Not for murder...not for being the spineless piece of shit you are."

He wrenched his head upwards, hate spewed from his eyes. "I'd do it again." He smiled. "I'd do it all again to end his miserable reign."

Salome's lips curled as a guttural growl ripped out. Her beast slipped closer to the surface, savagery spilling from her and then she swung.

The sickening tear of flesh made me look away. Kinraide choked and gasped, and then hit the cavern floor with a *thud.*

Julius and the rest of the Pride stepped closer, gathering around Arson.

"With this stone I'll be as real as you need." He looked at each Lion. "But Salome is your Queen. Salome will lead you. Salome will fight for you...she is who you need to turn to.'

It was hard to see her as anything but the woman I knew, ut as she turned toward her people, I could see the regal way she carried herself, and the way she never backed down...not even when her own life was at stake. "I was *never* running away from you." She stared at her pride. "I was giving myself a chance to survive...and find a way back to you."

"And you'll come with us now?" Julius met her gaze. "You'll return home."

Fingers grasped mine as Ava stared at Nesrin and then Salome.

There was a tiny shake of her head, as though she felt the same heart-filled pain Nesrin did. The Panther took a step closer, drawing Salome's gaze.

Heart and honor collided.

And the debris left behind was catastrophic.

"Yes, your Queen will go with you." Nesrin stared into the Lion's eyes and answered. "They're right, you were never meant to come here in the first place."

"Nesrin." Salome took a step forward and reached for her hand.

The soft, careful smile on the Panther's lips trembled, but there was no backing out of this. It seemed Kinraide had laid the trap after all, just in a way he never expected.

"You'll come and see me?" Salome whispered.

"Wild Lions couldn't keep me from you." Nesrin grasped her hand and forced a smile.

I turned away, feeling like I was prying into something that was far too personal to share, and met Judas' gaze. His lips curled at the sight of me. I gave Ava's hand a squeeze and then let her go.

Mine weren't the ones she needed to hold. She turned to Chuck as I stepped toward Judas and Nero. The seductive scent of Wolf washed over me as I stepped into their arms. I lifted my gaze, searching the open mouth of the cavern for Bond—but he still wasn't there.

"Where is Bond," I lifted my gaze to meet Judas' brown eyes.

"He's having a hard time lately." The Alpha reached up and brushed my hair. "But we'll find him, okay? We'll bring him home."

*Home.*

The word echoed inside me as I glanced back to Salome and Nesrin as they hugged.

It was time to say goodbye...time to step into a role she never expected.

*Just like me.*

"You ready to get out of here?" Judas murmured in my ear. "We find Bond, come back to my room...pick up where we left off the other night...."

A cold breeze skimmed across my skin. "First Bond," I answered. "First we find him, and then we'll see."

It was so easy for men like Judas to switch off. So easy to ignore the sadness and heartbreak. I glanced over to see Chuck and Ava heading for the entrance to the cave. Nesrin and Salome broke their embrace as two of the guards slapped the shackles on Kinraide. He kicked and bucked, earning a punch to the jaw....

Arson reached for Salome's hand and turned to Julius, and the faint words slipped through the air. "*I pledge to you my honor...as a man as well as a leader....*"

"Let's get back home." Chuck bent and heaved Ava into

the air, before throwing her over his shoulder. "I'm starving."

She just giggled, and reached down to slap his ass. "You've already eaten, *remember?*"

"Wasn't talking about that kind of starving...was I?"

I cringed as Chuck strode ahead in ground eating strides.

It was good to see him happy...good to see him as something other than the man I depended on. It was good to see him...*human.*

His footsteps thundered through the forest, trees swayed under the force.

Laughter slipped behind them.

And it seemed it was infectious. Judas grabbed my hand and gave me a wink. But it was Nero who pushed between us, stealing my hand with a cheeky smile before he leaned in, kissed me on the lips and pulled me with him.

We ran through the night, giggling like idiots in love.

I was an idiot in love.

Stars sparkled overhead as we leapt over thorny bushes and zig-zagged around thick clumps of trees. Judas ran beside me, eyes shining, lips curled. It seemed Bestias Academy had one less secret to cling to, and one less murderous-ghost chained to its grounds.

I only hoped that Salome's pride knew what they were in for with Brutus invading her...

Or maybe ignorance in this case really was bliss.

We broke through the tree line at the edge of Academy grounds and sucked in heavy breaths. Chuck and Ava were already cutting across the grounds towards the cottage, but they weren't laughing anymore...and Ava wasn't over his shoulder.

"Hellhounds," Judas snarled and glared into the night.

At the edge of the small house I saw them...three of them...and they were standing there, just staring...*at me*.

"If they came to fight the Lions, they're too damn late," Nero growled at my side. "Guards, my ass."

I followed Chuck and Ava, nearing the pavement that ran along the outside of the grounds as another man stepped around the edge of the building and into the light.

My heart lunged at the sight. "Nefarious?"

Panic filled me. Mom and Dad's faces filled my head as I picked up my pace. Chuck stilled in front of the teacher, and low, mumbled words reached my ears.

As my steps faltered and Judas growled a warning at my side...my Vampire guardian turned to face me. "Morwenna," he called.

But there was something in his eyes...something that whispered of *fear*.

"What is it?" My words were choked and strange. "What's wrong?"

Chuck shook his head and took a step toward me. His lips said one thing...*but his eyes were screaming another*.

"Slayer has come to Bestias Academy...."

*Run Morwenna...run now.*

"And he wants to see you...*alone*."

I stopped walked. Stopped feeling.

*Stopped existing* in that moment.

Slayer, the most brutal Vampire henchman to ever walk the earth spoke my name. If he was here, that only meant one thing....

*I was about to die.*

# EPILOGUE

Lights flickered overhead.

The stainless-steel table icy under my touch.

I stared at the two men standing across from me.

Two *mortal* men.

"I don't know why I'm here." Cold empty gazes stared back at me. "Can you at least let me call my parents?"

The yellow folder in one of the men's hands crumpled as he folded his arms. I'd been here for ages now...staring...waiting. I glanced at the door where Nefarious waited outside.

They wouldn't let anyone else come in not Chuck or Ava...or even the Wolves.

*Only me.* Nefarious glanced toward the Hellhounds from outside. *I'll be there...on behalf of the Ancient.*

That was fine...for the Ancient.

But who was here for me?

*Slayer...* The name pulsed inside my head. *Slayer. Slayer. Slayer.* I should've run, should've made them come to my dad. Should've demanded to be told why the henchman wanted me.

*Not to die.*

No. I lifted my gaze to the two mortals staring at me. He wouldn't bring me here...to this *foul,* haunting place. Footsteps echoed outside. Long strides. Heavy boots. Thunder, that's what it sounded like.

The two mortals in front of me shifted nervously and glanced at the door as the handle turned and Hell stepped inside.

Cold, calculating eyes skimmed over me. White hair seemed to reflect the fluorescent light. He never looked at the men, never looked at anything but me, and as he closed the door and rounded the stainless-steel table I realized—the center of this Vampire's attention was not somewhere I wished to be.

"Morwenna Livingstone."

He barely spoke, just a whisper. Still, I swallowed the whimper trapped in the back of my throat. Silver pupils were surrounded by night. Everything about him was contrast, long silver hair, black leather trenchcoat. Pale skin, and blood red lips. Lips that whispered of his last meal. I could smell blood on his breath, smell the rage in his veins. Smell his hunger.

Like it was rotting inside.

"That is your name, correct?"

I swallowed...again...and again and nodded. "I-I'd l-l-like to k-k-know why I'm-m here."

Dark brows pinched, pale skin furrowed as he leaned forward and placed his hands on the table in front of him. "You think I like being here?"

I shook my head.

"You think I like to deal with these...*these.*" Disgust sparkled in the silver of his eyes. I was entranced by the sight, by the ring of darkness around them as one of the mortal men behind him cleared his throat.

"That's not why you're here," one snapped.

The man stepped forward, unfurled his arms from across his body and cast the manila folder through the air to hit the table in front of me with a *slap*.

The corners of colored images spilled from its belly, as though the cardboard sheath clung tight to its secrets and didn't let go.

"I think you have something to tell me," Slayer whispered. "You know why I've come."

I shook my head as thoughts raced through my mind.

*Was it the Lions?*

*The Witches?*

*Was it the same Vampire group who had tried to kill my dad?*

Slayer reached over, and carefully, without a sound, flipped over the front cover of the folder.

Black and red filled my view, torn flesh, bloodied clothes. I stared at the dead body of a male and shook my head.

"Look closer."

The command was given as he slid the top photo across, revealing the one underneath.

Vacant eyes stared back at me.

*Familiar eyes.*

I lowered my gaze, taking in the open jacket as his face filled my mind. "I know him."

Slayer straightened as I leaned in. I lifted my hand and pulled the file close. "I know him..."

"Commissioner Neil Jordain," Slayer murmured. "You argued at a press conference not long ago, if I'm correct...*and now he's dead.*"

I jerked my gaze to his, fingers trembling as I pushed the photos away. "You don't think *I* did this?"

The Vampire henchman loomed over me. "I think you did this...*or you know who did.*"

We hope you enjoyed book four in our crazy, thrill-ride of a series. Relationships are growing stronger, but that hook for the next one. We're *brimming* with ideas and we can't wait to share them all with you.

Don't forget to join us in the Kila Foung Facebook group, we're posting extra scenes in there that you won't be able to find anywhere else.

See you there!

*Kim and Mila, a.k.a Kila Foung*

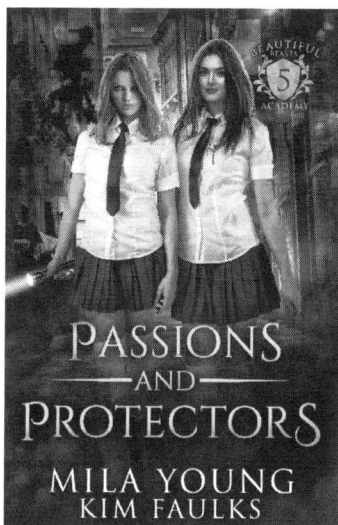

**Love is savage. Love is fierce. Love will stand beside you when the rest of the world turns their back. Love will claim its weapon of choice....my heart.**

There's a murderer on the loose...and mortals are calling for a name to bring to justice. A name that answers on behalf of the Ancient.

*My name...Morwenna Livingstone.*

My parents can't reach me.

My best friend doesn't even know where I've gone.

And as mortal deaths continue to plague Tricks City I'm called to stand before the tribunal of mortals and monsters and answer for the crime of conspiracy to murder.

Because I know who the real killer has been all this time.

I just couldn't bring myself to face him.

The betrayal.

The heartache...

And the end.

*Preorder your copy of Passions and Protectors here on Amazon*

Printed in Great Britain
by Amazon

68906910R00113